IN CARE OF
SAM BEAUDRY

BY
KATHLEEN EAGLE

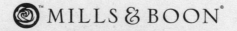

® MILLS & BOON®

First published in Great Britain 2010
Harlequin Mills & Boon Limited,
Eton House, 18-24 Paradise Road, Richmond, Surrey TW9 1SR

© Kathleen Eagle 2009

ISBN: 978 0 263 87969 8

23-0510

Harlequin Mills & Boon policy is to use papers that are natural, renewable and recyclable products and made from wood grown in sustainable forests. The logging and manufacturing processes conform to the legal environmental regulations of the country of origin.

Printed and bound in Spain
by Litografia Rosés S.A., Barcelona

Kathleen Eagle published her first book, an RWA Golden Heart Award winner, in 1984. Since then she has published more than forty books, including historical and contemporary, series and single title, earning her nearly every award in the industry, including a Lifetime Achievement Award from *Romantic Times BOOKreviews* and RWA's RITA® Award. Her books have consistently appeared on regional and national bestseller lists, including the *New York Times* extended bestseller list.

Ms Eagle lives in Minnesota with her husband, who is Lakota Sioux and a public school teacher. They have three children.

For my grandchildren

Chapter One

Sheriff Sam Beaudry knew when he was being watched. He could feel it on his skin, surpassing the threat of an itch from his overstarched brown and khaki shirt. Some people called it the creeps. For Sam it was *the eyeball crawl,* and it was taking place on the back of his neck, causing an increase in the pain his paperwork always caused him. This was what he got for sitting with his back to a window. But the square footage of the Bear Root County sheriff's office permitted only two ways to arrange a desk, and putting his back to the door was never an option. That was how Wild Bill had gotten himself plugged, as every fan of Western lore knew well.

The chair's casters squealed as Sam pushed back from the dependable old typewriter, reached for his brown stoneware mug and rose with deceptive ease.

The stiffness in his left knee would be walked off by the time he caught up with the eyeball's owner. *Never let 'em see you limp*. One corner of his mouth twitched as he took a moment to will the joint's battered ball to cozy up to its warped socket. *Or smile*.

The mug was another deception. Coffee wasn't what he was going for. It was bug-eyed surprise. He went out the front door, peered around the corner of the two-story brick building and silently drew an imaginary bead.

"Freeze!"

The boy sprang to attention, lost his grimy grip on the windowsill, his rubber-soled footing on the ledge, and tumbled backward into Sam's waiting arms.

"That means don't move, Jim." Sam lowered the sandy-haired spy to the ground and turned him around by his bony shoulders. "'Fraid I'm gonna have to take you in."

"How could I freeze?" Jimmy Whiteside looked up, tipping his head way back. He squinted one eye, even though Sam's shadow shielded him from the sun. "You 'bout scared the crap out of me."

"You keep that much under control, I might go easy on you." Sam checked his watch. "School ain't out yet. You're breakin' the law, boy."

"I didn't feel like going back inside after recess. It's hot in there."

"It's gonna be a lot hotter this afternoon when you're sittin' in detention."

The boy frowned. "What's detention?"

"What do they call it these days when you stay after school for punishment?"

"Staying after school. But mostly I get time out in the principal's office." Jimmy grinned. "I'm only in fourth grade."

"So you're what, nine?" Sam laid a hand on the boy's shoulder again. "In another year you'll be old enough to do hard time in Miles City, you keep on peekin' in people's windows. Especially when you're supposed to be in school." He squeezed slightly, gave the small shoulder a friendly shake. "*Hard time*, Jim. You know what that means?"

Jim rolled his shoulder and backed away. "It means you're trying to scare me."

Sam chuckled. He'd learned the art from his father's side. An Indian kid would know Sam's line for what it was—teasing with a blunt edge—and wouldn't have such a quick comeback. "Don't look now, but your mom's comin'."

The boy had ball bearings in his neck. Sam wanted to laugh, but with both of them watching the little woman in white take a little hop-skip across a curbside puddle and hit the Main Street pavement with pure purpose, he worked against it. "I warned you, Jim. Talk about scary."

Jim's head swiveled again, sporting a scowl this time, all for Sam. "What do you mean by that?"

"That woman means business. If I were you, I'd go quietly."

"Where?"

"Wherever she says." Sam nodded, keeping it serious. "Hey, Maggie. We were just—"

"Sam, I'm so sorry." She tucked a damp strand of honey-blond hair—which had escaped from her bobbing ponytail—behind her pixie ear. Her face was coated with a fine sheen, a testament to the workout her boy was given to putting her through. "Jimmy, I'm *so* upset. I thought we had an agreement." She drew a deep breath and treated Sam to an apologetic smile. "He's really interested in what you do. *Everything* you do." Hair secured, she planted small hand on sweet hip and drew down on the smile. "Mr. Cochran called me at work again, Jimmy. You can't just wander off the school grounds like that. Now you're in trouble with him *and* with me. And the sheriff, too." She glanced up with that uncomfortable smile. "I'm sorry, Sam."

"What about you, Jim?" he asked.

"Sorry." His face went down all hangdog, but it bobbed right back up guilt-free. "Carla Taylor said you shot a burglar in the shed behind the Emporium this morning. She saw you from the bus, and Lucky was barking like crazy."

"Yep. That dog comes by his name honestly. He was lucky he didn't get snakebit this morning."

"Carla said she heard you tell somebody to give himself up."

"Even a rattlesnake has rights."

Maggie laughed softly—a warm sound Sam would have gladly kept going if he could think of another good line.

But disappointment claimed the boy's freckled face. "I thought maybe you had a prisoner in there. Or a dead body."

"Nope." *Disappointment all around.* "But I got a nice set of rattles, which I'd be glad to show you next time you come around to the office. But not if you're climbin' around the window. And not when you're supposed to be in school." He laid a hand on Jim's shoulder. "You got yourself a double jeopardy situation here, Jim. I'm bowin' out. Apologies accepted." He nodded, reflexively raising his hand to the brim of the tan Stetson he wasn't wearing. "Maggie."

"Thanks, Sam."

Safe on the steps of the old county building, which housed his office downstairs and his second-floor apartment, Sam watched little Maggie Whiteside march her big-for-his-britches son across the street. The boy deserved credit for silently suffering a mother's hand-holding and hair-smoothing in full view of two stories of classroom windows, nodding dutifully in response to her words. Sam didn't know anything about Jim's father, but there must have been a father somewhere, and he must have been tall. Already a handful for a single mom, Jim didn't get his height from Maggie. But she had the upper hand.

A nurse at the Bear Root Regional Medical Clinic, Maggie was the kind of woman who talked like she knew you when she didn't, acted interested when she wasn't, and laughed like she was enjoying herself most of the time. It was cute, but mostly for show. Sam didn't know where she was from exactly—outside Montana there was only Back East and The Coast—but she'd only been living in Bear Root for about two years. Given time, she'd learn to cut the crap. Unfortunately, her kind of woman generally didn't take the time in Bear Root. Two years was stretching it.

Sam reached for the old brass knob on the front door just as one of the town's two sirens shattered the calm mountain air. *Distant, coming this way.* Either alarm served to galvanize every resident, but the Rescue Squad hit home hard and fast.

Is it my kid? My wife? My brother?

Sam was still watching Maggie, feeling the alarm along with her, the call to duty. She lifted her head as though there was an odor in the air, and she glanced back at him. *You smell that? It's big. It's bad.* They connected on the shared instinct.

Sam pulled his keys out of his pants pocket as he headed for the brown car emblazoned with a big, gold star. He felt a little light-headed, but it was only because he wasn't wearing his Stetson. Which meant he was out of uniform.

He started the car, flipped on the radio, noted Maggie's quick pace cutting across the schoolyard grass and mentally gave himself a demerit.

Lucky the Wonder Mutt learned fast.

It was his mistress who was a little slow on the uptake sometimes. But once Hilda Beaudry had the logistics figured out, Lucky's new trick was all but in the bag.

"Lucky, hit the lights."

The little black-and-white terrier—always a hit at Allgood's Emporium—jumped on cue, landed on the strategically placed footstool, and then sprang for the wall switch, hitting the target with his only front paw. Lucky could do more with three legs than most mutts could achieve on four. He didn't even need a command for the follow-up sit on the footstool. He perked his ears and waited prettily for his reward. Liver treats were his favorite. His long tongue curled around his nose as he whimpered.

"No, thank *you*. You're the one—"

"*Yip!*" Lucky's ears stood at attention. He tipped his head and stared past Hilda.

She turned. A small shadow darkened the bottom of the general store's old-fashioned screen door. "Do I have a customer, Lucky, or do you have an audience?"

"*Yip!*"

"Boy or girl?"

"*Yip!*"

"Oh, good. Your favorite." The shadow shifted. "And with free cookies for the first five people to come to the store today...how many so far?"

Hilda made the thumb signal for *speak* four times. Lucky cheerfully obliged.

"They're chocolate chi-i-ip," Hilda sang out.

The door's spring chirped in response, and a little girl with a long, droopy brunette ponytail and huge brown eyes stepped within view, toeing the threshold with a white rubber sneaker bumper.

At Hilda's signal, Lucky sat.

The child lifted her prim, pointed chin. "Do I have to buy anything?"

"In this store, free means free." And at Allgood's, chocolate chip meant recent business had been brisk. Hilda had a special recipe. Not for the cookies—she used the one on the chocolate-chip bag—but for the aroma. It was the scent that brought 'em in. She hadn't figured out how to bottle it, but the oscillating fan beside the kitchen window filled the air outside Allgood's Emporium with it.

"Come on in and help yourself. Two to a customer."

"But I'm not a customer."

It didn't really matter that the girl was holding the door open while she dithered betwixt and between, since spring hadn't sprung the worst of the flying insects yet.

Lucky's throaty warble came on the heels of Hilda's invitational gesture. "Introduce yourself and we'll become friends. Friends get three, but you have to take the third one home for later."

"We don't live here." With one hand behind her back the girl eased the door shut. "I've never seen a dog turn on a light. How come he only has three legs?"

"That's all he needs."

"Was he born that way?"

"I don't know for sure." Hilda put her hands on her hips and eyed the dog. "He was this size when he came to live with me, and we liked each other right off. We've never talked about our ages or what shape we're in. What you see is what you get." She looked up at the girl. "Does it seem warm to you? Lucky, turn on the fan for us, please."

The terrier needed three strategically placed stools— small, medium, tall—to reach the counter under the long pull-string on the ceiling fan.

The dimension of the girl's eyes rounded up to the next size. "Wow."

"Are you here visiting, or just passing through?"

"We came on the bus. We're staying at the Mountain Mama Motel. My mom likes the name, but I don't like the way that arrow blinks on and off at night. It keeps us awake." She stared at the plate Hilda had pushed under her nose, and then glanced up. Hilda nodded, but the girl needed more than a nod, more than a cookie. "My…my mom's really sick."

"Is it just the two of you?" The girl nodded. "How long has she been sick?"

"A little bit for a long time, but she's getting worse."

"Would you like me to go see her? I have a good friend who's a nurse. We can—"

"My name's Star Brown." She took the top cookie, tasted it and daintily brushed a gathering of crumbs from her bottom lip. "My grandmother owns this store."

"I own this store, honey, and I really wish I had a granddaughter. But I'm afraid—"

"Is your name Hilda Beaudry?"

"It is." Her name was painted on the sign above the overhang out front. Small letters, but she'd matched them to her father's and grandfather's names, which were still there with their dates as proprietors.

"We came here to find you. My mom says grandmothers are mothers, too. But just older because their sons and daughters are fathers and mothers now."

"I always wanted a daughter, but I only have sons, and they have no…" The child looked confused, disappointed, as though she was expecting someone who didn't show up or her goldfish had stopped moving. Hilda didn't like being the bearer of bad news. "Why don't we go check on your mother? We'll put up the BS sign. *Back Soon*."

"You're the only grand—" Star went still at the sound of a siren.

"That sound says 'Make way for the Bear Root Rescue Squad.'"

"What's that?"

"It's our ambulance." Hilda moved toward the door as another warning siren rose like a mating call to the first one. They screamed in tandem, coming on hard until they blew past the store—*yeeee-ooooow whoop-whaaa*—drawing down on the end of Main. Not much left on that end besides… "Headed for the motel."

Star barreled through the screen door like a ball aimed at the last pin standing.

Hilda started after her but reversed course at the sound of scrabbling claws. "Leave it! Come." The dog did his three-paw jig across the threshold and passed his mistress. "Can't trust you for a minute with the smell of chocolate in your nose."

Hilda glimpsed the dropped piece of cookie on the floor as the door swung shut. She had that part of the job mastered. She could make a damn fine cookie. At the edge of the yard the girl's hair was swinging like a metronome as she sprinted into the street after the sheriff's car.

Sam?

She couldn't be Sam's. Zach's, maybe, but not…

Hilda's boot heels rattled down the wooden steps.

"Come on, Lucky. Follow that ponytail."

Chapter Two

Maggie shooed Jimmy through the heavy glass door ahead of her. Stern-faced principal Dave Cochran greeted her with a nod, the better part of his attention fixed on the approaching ambulance. The siren crashed through Maggie's head, in the left ear, out the right, tugging on her like a knotted thread.

"Looks like they're headed for the motel," the principal said, eyes glued to the action. "Dr. Dietel is looking for you, Jimmy. Tell her you already saw me."

"I'm sorry, Mr.—"

"Be in my office at three-thirty. Get to class now." He craned his neck toward the glass, the very image of a long-legged blue heron getting ready to take off. "Don't think anyone's staying there. Didn't see any cars this morning. Hope it's not Mama Crass."

"Or Teddy. I'm going to run on down there and see

if they need help." She hadn't gone for her daily jog yet. Halfway out the door, she hesitated, caught between duties, leaning toward escape. "Unless you want to talk to me. Jimmy was hanging around Sam's office again."

"Sam shouldn't encourage—"

"I'll stop back." She backpedaled until the door left her fingertips and slowly swung shut. "Or call, depending. Consequences at school, consequences at home. Team effort." She gave him a thumbs-up through the glass.

The principal cracked a smile. A good sign for Jimmy. Maggie knew at least two things about this man—he was attracted to her, and he liked being quoted. The first was unsettling. Dave was two things that didn't interest her: old and married. The second was useful. Since she probably wouldn't be able to "stop back," the homage to the last discipline lecture he'd given her was a sacrifice in behalf of her son's defense. She didn't condone Jimmy's actions, but it wasn't like he was leaving school grounds to go on a crime spree. He wanted to be Sam Beaudry.

Maggie jogged across the graveled parking area toward the flashing lights of the now silent ambulance. Driver Dick Litelle was opening the back doors while motel owners Cassie and Ted Gosset took turns jumping in and out of the emergency team's way as they directed Dick's partner, Jay, toward the cause for concern.

"She called the desk, but I couldn't tell—"

"She said she couldn't get up, didn't she?" Teddy put in, shifting his negligible weight anxiously as though he worried about getting blamed for something. "I told Mama to check on her, but she had to go... You had to go fix your hair first! Just the woman and her little girl checked in, so I didn't wanna—"

"Need any help?"

"Yeah, hey, Maggie." Dick made a be-my-guest gesture in the direction of door number three. "I'll bring the gurney. Ted, Cassie, let Maggie through."

"She's the skinniest woman I ever saw," claimed Cassie, who had applied considerable effort to keeping her own weight up. "Not you, Maggie," Mama Crass hastened to explain as she nodded toward number three. "The one in there."

"What's her name?" Maggie called out over her shoulder.

"Is the little girl in there?" Cassie called toward the open door. "You should send her out."

"The woman's name," Maggie insisted.

"Merilee Brown," said Teddy.

"The little one shouldn't be in there watching," Cassie said, lifting her voice to whomever would listen.

The room was dark and smelled like rancid potato chips and sweat. "Hey, sweetie," Maggie called out, glancing toward the bathroom as she moved to the side of the bed opposite Jay. "There's a child," she whispered. She raised her voice. "We're going to take you and your mommy for a ride in a big van."

"She's got a pulse, but it's pitiful," Jay reported from the bedside, where Maggie joined him. With space at a premium, he stepped aside, deferring to the unofficial top-of-the-pecking-order designation Maggie's skills had earned her in the two years since she'd been on staff.

"Merilee, can you hear me? We're here to help you." Maggie directed Jay toward the bathroom door, which stood open. He knew what to look for. "Where's your little girl, Merilee? What's her name?"

"What's she saying?"

"Sounds like she's counting. Did you take pills, Merilee?" Maggie leaned close to the woman's pale lips, fingers on the thready pulse. At her back, Dick was raising the gurney. "Anything, Jay?"

"Not much." Jay came out of the bathroom brandishing a small plastic bag. "Meds. No kid."

"Check under the beds." Maggie tucked a white blanket around the patient while Dick strapped her down. "I'll ride with her."

Sam watched Dick Litelle back through door number three, pulling the loaded gurney out after him. The patient came out feetfirst, swaddled like a mummy. Sam endured a few seconds of dry-mouthed suspense before getting his first glimpse of a frowsy head with unopened eyes and uncovered face—not dead, but deathly pallid—as it slid into the sunlight. The translucent frailty of a once hard-edged beauty now stung his eyes. *Merilee Brown.* The name the Gossets had given him was a surprise, but the face was a shocker. The years were written on it a thousand times over.

"Mommy!"

Sam spun on his heel.

"They're taking my mom!"

"Wait, honey."

Sam jerked his head toward the sound of a voice more familiar than his own. Sure enough, his mother was there, wrapping her arms around a child who had suddenly become her *honey*. The same child claiming Merilee for her mom.

Hilda looked up at him, her chest heaving as she

struggled to catch her breath. "Sam, what's happened? This little girl just showed up at the—"

"Merilee Brown." A flurry of disconnected images—some sweet, some sordid—swirled behind Sam's staring eyes. "I used to…" He shook his head hard and got his wits back in line. "Ted says she called the front desk and said she couldn't get up. Says his wife went to the room right away and found her like this." He got his feet moving as Maggie hopped into the ambulance as soon as the stretcher was in place. "I'll clear the way," he called to the driver.

His mother grabbed his arm. "This is her daughter."

His glance ping-ponged between the two faces—Ma, kid, Ma—and he jerked open the back door of his patrol car. "Let's go."

Sam shut off the lights in the back of his mind. He moved quickly. Siren, radio contact, eyes on the street, head in the moment. His mother knew better than to speak to him on the way to Bear Root Medical. The dizzying *whoosh* from here to there made for insulated silence within the car, wailing without.

It wasn't until they were back on foot, following the gurney through the emergency entrance like three spellbound pilgrims, that Sam's thoughts got personal again. *Merilee had come to Bear Root.* He glanced at the top of the little head bobbing along between him and his mother. *She'd brought a kid with her.*

What the *hell?*

He called the office to check in with Phoebe Shooter, his deputy, told her to "woman the fort" and then stationed himself in a chair with a view. Had everything covered—the door to the ICU, the nurse's station, the outside world through a window in the lobby down the hall…everything except what he was getting paid for. He should have been finishing the paperwork he'd left on his desk so he could take a ride out to the abandoned Osterhaus place and check out Minnie Lampert's umpteenth sighting of "suspicious activity." Any change with Merilee, he'd get a call from somebody. His mother was hovering over the girl like they were cuffed to each other, and they'd both been admitted to the room with Merilee.

Was that a bad sign?

"Where was the little girl?"

Sam turned toward the welcome sound of Maggie's voice. Her question didn't register, but the just-between-us look in her green eyes did. She handed him a warm foam cup with a plastic lid as she settled into the chair next to his. "We were looking for her in the motel room," she explained.

"At the store, I guess." He peeled back the tab on the plastic lid. "Ma has a way with strays."

"Strays? That's an odd—"

"Looks like she strayed off to the store and left her mother in a bad way without any…" He trailed off on a sip of black coffee.

"She's just a little girl, Sam." She glanced toward the door marked Intensive Care as she took a drink from her own cup. "Where are they from? Do the Gossets know anything about the woman?"

"Merilee Brown," he said quietly.

"Other than what's on the registration card."

"I don't know what's on the registration card. She used to work at a truck stop in Wyoming. She moved to California eight, close to nine years ago."

"You know her?"

She sounded startled. Like she didn't know he'd ever been outside Bear Root County. Not that they'd ever talked about his travels. Generally, that was where his mother came in, talking up his so-called adventures.

"I didn't know she was here in town. Can't imagine what she'd be doing here." He braced his elbows on his knees, cradled the coffee between his hands and studied the jagged hole in the lid. "Is it drugs?"

"I don't know," she said solemnly. "Jay found some meds, but I didn't see what they were. Does she use?"

"She did when I knew her. I haven't seen her since I joined the marines. How bad off is she?"

"It doesn't look good. They took her to X-ray."

Maggie settled back in her chair. Her white skirt crept a few inches above her knees. The other nurses wore white pants, but not Maggie. He couldn't figure out whether she was old-fashioned or she just liked dresses better. She looked good in a dress, even if it was a uniform, but she might have blended in a little better if she wore pants.

Or not. Maggie was different, no doubt about that. Blending wasn't her way. Not that he was an authority on the ways of Maggie Whiteside, but he'd taken considerable notice. Thought a lot about studying up.

"Were you close?" she asked.

He pushed up on his thigh with the heel of his hand and questioned her with a look.

"Well, she's lying there unconscious, and nobody else around here seems to know her. Just you."

"It's been a lotta years, Maggie, what can I tell you? She did weed, coke, pills and I don't know what else, but I never saw her like this." He gave a jerk of his chin. "And she didn't have any kids. How old is—"

He squared up at the sight of his mother rounding the corner of the hallway just past ICU with a reluctant little girl in tow. The child homed in on Nurse Maggie, downshifted for traction and marched past the nurse's station like a little soldier, all business. "They took my mom somewhere, but they won't tell me what's wrong with her. Do you know?"

"Not yet, sweetie. The doctor's trying to figure that out right now."

"Can't she wake up?"

"The doctor's working on getting her to wake up. Has she been sick very long?"

"I don't know. I mean, I think so. I know she was sick on the bus. She doesn't like to ride the bus. She said she'd be better after she got to sleep in a bed for a while." She turned and stared at the ICU door. "Why can't I stay with her?"

"Because the doctor wants us all out of the way for right now. He's the one who can help your mom, but he needs room to maneuver." Maggie scooted to the edge of her chair and touched the back of her lanky little arm, testing. "I know it's hard to wait."

Tension melted visibly from the small shoulders as Maggie's hand stirred, but still the girl stared as though she could see through walls. "What's he doing to her?"

"They're taking pictures. Do you know what an X-ray is?"

"Yes. I had one on my arm last year."

"After the doctor's finished, they'll bring her back to that same room, which is where we take extra special care of our patients. You'll be able to see her again for a few minutes. I'll make sure." Maggie stood, sliding her hand over the girl's shoulder as security against her promise. "Are you hungry?"

An attendant appeared and called Maggie's number with a gesture. She patted the little girl's shoulder. "Hilda, would you take…"

"Star," Hilda supplied.

"…Star to the lounge and get her something to eat?"

Once Star was out of earshot, Maggie turned to Sam. "Did the woman come looking for you?"

"You'll have to ask her."

She stared at him for a moment as though she thought he had more answers than he'd given. Like he'd ever known what was on Merilee's mind, which was why he answered the way he did. He wasn't being a smart-ass.

But Maggie must have thought so. She distanced herself with a step, a look and a tone. "Let's hope we get the chance."

Sam nodded, but Maggie turned from him and missed it. She had nursing to do.

Hoping had never helped much where Merilee was concerned, but he was willing to give it another shot at Maggie's suggestion. Hope she could beat whatever this was and come back to her kid. Meanwhile he had to figure out who the hell he should notify if hope didn't fly. Heading for his car, he thought up one more hope— that the person to contact in Merilee's behalf didn't turn out to be Vic Randone.

He checked in at the office and then took a run out to the Osterhaus place, which was tucked into the foothills just below the little high country town of Bear Root. Old Bill Osterhaus had been dead more than a year, and his relatives had sold what little stock and equipment he'd had, but they were still fighting over what to do with the property. His neighbor, Minnie, who was as old as the hills with a head twice as hard, had visions of "squatters" moving in. Sam stopped in to let the old woman know that the only squatters he'd found this time were four-legged, but that she should call him whenever she had concerns. He meant it. Hell, she was a voter.

He meant to drive right on past the hospital when he got back into town, but he hadn't heard any news, and it was just as easy to stop as call, especially on the chance there had been some improvement. He found Merilee—or the shell of Merilee—alone in the cool, antiseptic-smelling, closely monitored room. He strad-dled a chair, rested his forearms over the backrest, listened to a soft rush of air and a machine's rhythmic beep. Watching her pale purple eyelids twitch, waiting for something else to stir, wondering what, if anything, was going on inside that crazy head—oh, yeah, he'd been there before.

"What's goin' on, Merilee?" He stacked his fists end to end and rested his chin in the curl of his thumb and forefinger. "Tell me. Maybe I can—" *damn your thick head, Beaudry, don't even think it* "—help."

Saying it was even worse than thinking it. Luckily, the only other ears in the room seemed to be shut down.

"But who knows, huh? Maybe you can hear me, so…well, your little girl's safe. She's a beauty. Looks just like you. I haven't had a chance to talk to her much.

Didn't wanna scare her with a lot of questions right off. Is she old enough to tell me what's goin' on?"

He glanced at the monitor that made her heartbeat visible. A blip on the radar. She had that much going on. For now.

"Anyway, she's with my mother. I told you about Ma. She runs the store here. I can't remember what all I told you about Bear Root. Back when I met you, I thought I'd left home for good." He straightened his back, drew a deep breath just to be sure he could and sighed. "Live and learn, huh?" He reached for her hand.

He'd lived ten years and learned many more hard lessons since his roughneck days, knocking around the Western oil fields with Vic Randone, the buddy he'd met up with in Alaska. He'd gone from knocking around to being knocked out—almost literally—by a beautiful, butterfingered waitress in a Wyoming truck stop. Merilee Brown. Talk about a knockout. The ghost of a woman nearly lost in hospital-bed sheets and struggling for every ventilated breath wasn't much more than a sliver of the vibrant girl Sam remembered. His first glimpse of her laughing face had been branded into his brain. She'd slopped some water on the floor behind his chair—got him in the back with it, but he didn't mind—and then came back and slipped in it and conked him over the head with a tray. He'd caught her and fallen for her in the same instant.

Merilee, Merilee, Merilee, Merilee, life is but a dream.

She was magic. She could be silly one moment and thoughtful the next. She wore her heart on her sleeve, but she changed it with her clothes. She was passionate about being passionate, and her passion show never failed to captivate Sam. She could get just as excited about the color of an apple as the purchase of a much-needed pair of shoes. She made no apologies for doing what she had to do to get what she wanted, but she gave easily, and she never kept score. She was everything Sam wasn't, didn't have the makings or the means to be, but always wondered what it would be like. Rubbing shoulders with magic was one way to find out.

Vic hadn't been with him at the truck stop that day, but he was never far away, and it wasn't long before they'd become a threesome. On the outside they were three carefree pals stopping over in Wyoming on their way to the rest of their lives. But on the inside, there were cares. Big, bad, unbearable cares. Merilee cared for living on the edge. Vic cared for money. Sam, who had cared for getting out of Bear Root, now cared for Merilee. With cares safely stowed in their separate little bags they'd left Wyoming for California, where Vic made some easy money, Merilee made some edgy choices, and Sam eventually made peace with becoming the odd man out by doing what generations of Indian men before him had done. He'd enlisted.

"And living with you and Vic, I sure learned." With his thumb he sketched a slow circle on the back of her hand. "No regrets. A guy's gotta get educated somehow."

He fixed his eyes on the cool, thin hand lying in his—a china trinket on a wooden shelf. He had to force himself to look at what was no more than a mask of the face that had once left him breathless. He ought to regret leaving her, but he didn't. He couldn't. Worse, he wanted to get up and leave her now. It hurt to look at her. She was in a bad way, and he could do nothing to undo whatever had been done. He wasn't a doctor or a miracle worker or a magician. He was, like any man worth his salt, a guardian. And like any man who could survive on little more than the salt that measured his worth, he'd made keeping the peace his life's work.

"So why are you here, Merilee? You didn't want anything from me when you could've…" He shook his head. So he'd had some regrets, carried them around for a while, but not anymore. He couldn't remember exactly when he'd last thought about her. "Why now?"

Because she's dying now, and she has a kid.

Where had that come from? *Dying?* Hell, she'd made it to a hospital and gotten fixed up before. She'd do it again. She was young. And, yeah, she had a kid. She had something to live for besides Merilee.

The last time he'd seen her, it was all about Merilee. And Vic, she'd told Sam, she was "so into Vic." Sam had actually tried not to see any of it coming. The drugs were their business. Maybe they'd been busier with their business lately, but he was pretty sure it was mostly weed. Harmless weed. Was that what was making them bug-eyed and jumpy and downright mean lately?

No, that was *him*. He was always on their case about "taking the edge off the day" the way everybody did, with a pipe or a little blow. They had it under control. Besides, Sam wasn't exactly a saint. And they weren't shutting him out. There was plenty of everything to go around.

Back then it was all about Merilee.

She'd looked bad the day he left, but not this bad. Not

death's-door bad. "You're such a good man," she'd said. "I'm doing you a favor. You're doing *yourself* a favor. The marines build men, you know. I take them apart, piece by piece."

She'd been right. After Merilee, boot camp had been a piece of cake.

But seeing her this way reminded him of his tour in the Middle East. He couldn't wrap his mind around it, so he sucked it up—mind, body, soul—and packed it all in tight around his heart.

Chapter Three

Hilda topped off Dave Cochran's sack of groceries with a plump loaf of Wonder Bread, put his card number through her new dial-up system and watched Star sneak Lucky an unearned treat while the phone sweet-talked a distant computer into approving the principal's purchase.

"Is your school on break?" Dave asked absently as he slipped his wallet into his back pocket.

"Star's visiting with her mother," Hilda explained. She wasn't sure what had roused her defensive instincts. Principals probably went to sleep at night counting children instead of sheep.

"What grade are you in, Star?" was his automatic follow-up.

"Second."

"Mr. Cochran's the principal of our school."

"You only have one school?"

"The older kids go to Bear Root Regional, which is over in Medicine Hat. But our second graders go to Mr. Cochran's school. The second grade teacher is…"

"We have two for second grade," Dave said. "Mr. Wilkie and Miss Petrie. How many do you have?"

"Four, but there's another whole school over on Water Street. I could go to either one. Can I give Lucky another treat?"

"Only for another trick. Star's from…" Hilda dragged the dog treat jar across the counter and poised to spin the cap. "What's the name of your town, honey?"

Star sprang out of her Lucky-level crouch as though she'd been bitten. "I think I should go back to the hospital now, in case my mom's awake yet."

"We'll have some supper here in a minute." Hilda handed Dave his credit card. "There you go, Mr.… Oh, look who's here," she chirped, echoing the spring on the screen door.

Dave greeted Maggie and her son in his principal's voice. Maggie was polite. Jimmy was quiet, clearly on a short leash. There was a brief exchange about the boy's behavior during the second half of the day as Mr. Cochran turned on what passed for his charm. Hilda took pleasure in seeing for herself that Maggie didn't get it. Or didn't appear to. The pheromones were missing the target.

Hilda had heard plenty of comments about Maggie's eligibility—single women were harder to find in Bear Root than available men—and she'd been treated to more than a few silly imitations of Dave Cochran's stiff-necked approach. The real thing would have been more painful than gratifying to watch if Hilda hadn't mentally taken Maggie off the mate market. On so many levels, Maggie was taken. All she and Sam had to do was wake up and smell the music.

"Yes, sir, I promise," Jimmy was saying, and Cochran offered an awkward high five. Some people shouldn't do high fives, Hilda thought. She, being an old lady, was probably one of those people, and the school principal, being the school principal, was certainly another.

"We appreciate your patience," Maggie called after him.

"Just don't tell him his call is important to you," Hilda whispered. "He'll think you mean it."

Maggie shot her a look before turning her attention to their new charge. "Hey, Star, I see you've made friends with the star attraction of Allgood's Emporium." She bent to pat the motor-tailed little dog, quietly adding, "I just came from the hospital. Your mom's still resting, and Dr. Dietel is taking good care of her."

"I wanna go see her. She'll be waking up pretty soon."

"I thought we'd have a little supper first," Hilda said. There was more to it than food, of course. There was company. Acting on the theory that kids help each other cope, Maggie had offered to bring her son over for supper. With a hand on each child's shoulder, Hilda made a bridge of herself. "This is Jimmy. He's just about your age."

"How old are you?" Jimmy challenged. "I'm nine."

"I'm seven and a half."

"I'm nine and—" he used his fingers to calculate "—seven months, so you're way younger."

Star looked up at Hilda and murmured plaintively, "I'm not hungry."

"Your mom would worry if she knew you weren't eating. I know I would." And did. It was easier than worrying about the faces of Star's comatose mother and her own uneasy, unforthcoming son. She slipped her arm around the girl's shoulders. "And you're worried about her. I know I would. So we'll all go upstairs, sit down and have some food, and then we'll go see her."

"Will she get well?"

"Dr. Dietel is very good at finding out what's wrong and making it right," Maggie put in. Hilda nodded, giving her friend the keep-talking look as she flipped the sign on the door to Closed. "He's still working on the first part, but she's getting two things we all need. Food and water."

"If she could eat she'd be awake," Star reasoned. "Did she wake up at all?"

"Not yet, but she's getting her food put directly into her body through a tube."

"And we have to put yours through your mouth." Hilda made a sweeping gesture toward the stairway to the heavenly scent of her famous Hilda's Crock-Pot Cacciatore.

"Mmm, smells like our favorite." Maggie extended a come-with-me hand to Star. "And tomorrow, maybe you'd like to go to school with Jimmy. Just for a little while. Visit Mom for a little while, maybe have lunch with me."

"I'll ask my mom." Star accepted Maggie's hand. "Tomorrow, when she wakes up."

Hilda served her guests at the table that had been in her kitchen since she'd taken over the store, basically the same kitchen she'd grown up in, although she'd replaced the woodburning stove with gas right after her father died. Daddy had refused to depend on anything he couldn't harvest with his own hands. Not that he didn't use store-bought—he ran a store, after all—but using and depending were two different things. Hilda had moved the stove downstairs and made it part of the country store décor. Her kitchen was still cozy, and any number of power failures and stranded gas trucks had given her pause to appreciate the little potbelly wood burner she'd kept in the living room when she was "updating." Her TV was a little dated, but she didn't have much time to watch it, anyway. She did love to cook, and she wished she had room for a bigger table and more guests.

Hilda got a charge out of sitting Maggie in Sam's place. She'd had them figured for a match ever since she'd met Maggie, who would surely charge Sam up a bit, while he would offer her some good ol' Western grounding. Every time those two came within sight of each other, you could already feel the current flowing.

After supper, Lucky lured the children into the living room while Maggie helped Hilda clean up the supper dishes.

"Is her mother going to wake up?" Hilda asked quietly as she slid four scraped plates into the mound of bubbles Maggie was growing in the sink.

"You've heard of trying to get blood from a stone? That poor woman. It'd be easier to get an IV into Mount Rushmore." Maggie flipped the faucet handles and lowered her voice in the new quiet. "Has Sam been able to get in touch with her family?"

"I haven't had much chance to talk with him, but I'm sure he's trying. I guess he knows her pretty well." She glanced up at Maggie. "Or *did*."

"You don't?"

"Never even heard the name." She pulled a beats-me face. "My boys used to tell me everything when they were Jimmy's age."

Maggie glanced over her shoulder at the sound of one quick bark and two easy laughs. "When did they stop?"

"I've never asked. I'm satisfied with the way I remember it. They told me everything back then. Anything they don't tell me now, I probably don't need to know."

"Until you do."

"And then they'll tell me. Sam will, anyway." Soon, she hoped. "It all works itself out. Ninety-five percent of your worries never materialize, and four out of the other five turn out to be a whole lot less dire than you thought."

"That leaves one percent."

"Yes, it does. And that's life."

Maggie screwed her head and rested her chin on her shoulder to get another look at her son. "Math was never my strong suit, but it sounds like I could improve his chances by increasing the worries."

"You're absolutely right." Hilda met Maggie's questioning glance with a smile. "Math is not your strong suit."

"I'm not the best worrier, either. I don't want Jimmy to get shortchanged just because I'm a single parent."

"That small percent is always gonna be there no

matter how many parents a kid has. You can throw yourself in front of the bus, but he could still get hit."

Maggie chuckled. "That's what I like about you, Hilda. You never give away the ending."

"Speaking of which, have you finished the book for this week?" Hilda pulled a paperback novel off the top of the refrigerator. "Who suggested this, anyway? The wrong guy gets the girl."

"Well, *now* I've finished it."

"Just kidding." She set the book aside. "Mr. Right always gets the girl. And Mr. Lucky gets—"

The dog barked. Hilda laughed, but he barked again. And again. She turned to the kitchen door just as it opened and the brim of a hat appeared. "It's just me, Ma."

"And you missed supper, but there's some left."

"Thanks, I'm good." Sam acknowledged Maggie with a nod and took his hat off in one economical gesture as he closed the door behind him. "I still have some paperwork to finish up. Kinda lost track of some of the details."

"It's caccia-to-reee," Hilda sang out. She knew he hadn't eaten. As hard as she'd tried to feed him up, he was still as skinny as he was when he'd come home from the service.

"Smells great. If it's gone tomorrow, you'll know I got the midnight munchies." He held up a big plastic bag. "One of the nurses said you'd taken charge of the little girl, so I brought over a few things that were in the room."

Star's little head rose above the dog-kid huddle like a periscope. "What room?"

"The motel room." Sam cleared his throat, eyeing the child as though he was afraid he might scare her. Or she, him. Quietly he explained, "I thought you might need some clothes."

"Where's my backpack?"

"It's safe in my office. I'm…" He shifted to a lower voice, his version of theatrical. "I'm the sheriff in these parts, so I get to—"

"You can't have my backpack. All my stuff is in it."

"I'm not going to keep it. Listen…Star?" He looked to Hilda for approval, and she nodded. *That's right, son. You're doing fine.* He squatted on his heels, hat on his knee, and offered the child the plastic bag. "Star, can you tell me where you and your mother live now? And how you got here?"

She peered into the bag. "We used to live in California, but not anymore." She pulled her face out of the bag and told Sam, "We came on the bus to find my grandmother."

"Where does your grandmother live?" he asked, his voice soft and gentle.

"Right here."

Sam looked up at Hilda as though she was the one who owed an explanation.

"I need your help downstairs, Sam." She nodded toward the door. "Can't quite reach the Oreos. Maggie, would you give the kids some ice cream while Sam helps me get the cookies?" She glanced at Star. "And then we'll go check on your mom. Okay?"

Hilda said nothing as she led the way downstairs, followed by one of only two people in the world that could make her a real grandmother. Strong, steadfast, straight-shooting Sam. Hilda marched past the cookies and turned on him between cough drops and condoms.

"I don't know what she's doing here, Ma." Hat in hand, he made a helpless gesture, all innocence. "It's been more than eight years since I last saw her. Met her down in Wyoming when I was workin' the oilfields. We were together for a while before I enlisted."

"Star tells me I'm the grandmother she came looking for."

Stared for a long moment, and then shook his head. "I don't think so."

"You don't *think* so."

"I left because there was another man."

"Who's my competition?"

"Mrs. Randone, I guess. Vic never said much about his family, but whoever raised him, she'd be no match for you, Ma. On the other hand, I wasn't the right match for Merilee."

"You never looked back?"

He lifted one strapping shoulder. "I called her a couple of times after I left. Wanted to make sure she was all right. I let her know I was shippin' out. She didn't say anything about a kid. She barely said anything at all."

"Star's last name is Brown," Hilda reminded him.

A long moment passed over that thought. No father. Exclusively her mother's child. Hilda knew her son, knew they were chewing on the same tough truth. Somebody hadn't done his job.

"I just talked to the doctor. She's in real bad shape." Sam glanced toward the top of the stairs. "How's the girl doin'? Does she seem okay?"

"Considering she's in a strange place and her mother's laid up in some kind of a coma, I think she's doing pretty well." She laid her hand on her boy's

sleeve. "She's a brave little girl. Quite grown up for one
so young. She cares wholeheartedly for her mother."

He drew a deep breath and blew a sigh, still staring.
"Merilee did a lot of drugs. That was another reason I
left. If she was pregnant and still into…" He looked to
his mother for assurance. "The girl seems, you know…
really okay?"

"Her name is Star."

"I found her birth certificate in Merilee's stuff.
'Father unknown' looks pretty cold when you see it in
black and white. I don't know anything about Merilee's
family. As for Randone…" He shook his head. "I don't
know, Ma. You ask me, he shouldn't be anybody's
father, but he was…you know."

Under different circumstances, his reluctance to put
it into words for his mother would have amused her.
He'd had sex with a woman. Not that the fact that somebody had been having sex with her, too, was amusing,
but he couldn't tell her in so many words. She was his
mother. And he was forever Sam.

"Your woman brought her child here, son. Star knew
my name. She knew about the store."

"I can't claim she was ever really my woman, but I
told Merilee all kinds of things."

"Good things?"

"She came lookin' for you, didn't she?" He gave her
a loving smile. "I'm always talkin' you up, Ma."

"You're not what I'd call a big talker," she teased, and
he suffered in silence as she patted his chiseled jaw. "It
has to be you, Sam. You're the one she was looking for.
Had to be. Maybe she thought you were still in the
marines all this time."

"Wouldn't be hard for her to find that out without coming here." He reached around her and plucked a package of Oreos off the shelf. "Especially if she told them she had my kid. The military's pretty fussy about stuff like that."

"Well, we're speculating. We can do the detective work later. Right now I seem to have a granddaughter."

"Yeah, well, don't get too attached." He handed her the cookies.

"I'm going to take Star at her word, Sam. Her mother's word. That's all she has to hang on to right now. The little security the child has."

Staring at the top of the stairs once again, Sam pressed lips together and nodded mechanically. "You're a nice lady, Hilda Beaudry."

"Nice has nothing to do with it. I'm a woman of grandmothering age, and all I have is unattached sons. My clock is ticking, and I'm realizing I could actually have grandchildren, and they could be anywhere."

"I take back *nice*."

"I already gave it back." But not her new role. "Who's going to decide where she stays?"

"Social services, and I've already talked to them. Lila Demery's the social worker assigned to the hospital. Until somebody else comes forward, I'm the only one who knows Merilee, and since I'm the sheriff…" He raised an eyebrow and returned the pat on the cheek. "I'm going to leave Star with you for now. But put the clock in a drawer."

"I told her we'd have supper and then go see her mother." He questioned her judgment with a look. "It's what she wants. She's already seen the worst."

"I'm givin' you *wise*. You're a wise woman, so I guess you know what you're doin'."

"That's better than nice. I'm old enough, I don't have to be nice."

"It's good Maggie brought her kid over. Kids do better with other kids around."

"Maggie has good instincts." She gave a perfunctory smile. "Come up and have something to eat, and then we'll all go see—"

He stepped back. "Naw, I'll meet you at the hospital. It's touch-and-go, and I don't want the girl to walk in at a bad time."

Hilda nodded. Her son had good instincts, too.

Sam had a duty here. It was a word he understood, and he carried it into the hospital room with him like the badge he wore on his shirt every day. There was no doubt about duty, no pondering risks or considering alternatives or seeking shelter. He'd once loved the woman, and the child was hers. For the moment, they had no one else. It was his duty to take care of them somehow. The *somehow* part was a little vague, but it wasn't operative. *Duty* was operative.

Wasn't it? Or was it *care?*

No, *taking* care, that would be his action. They would be in his care, and he would take steps. He wasn't much for walking softly—so said his boot heels whomping across the tile in the otherwise eerie quiet—but he would see to their needs.

Whatever Merilee needed, she wasn't saying. As promised, he'd met her visiting party in the lobby and given the go-ahead. Merilee was hanging in there. Hilda took Star into the room, but she soon stepped out and ordered him to trade places with her. "She's alone in a strange world. At least tell her you know her mother," she told him. "She needs to talk to someone who has that in common with her."

It was a scary assignment for a man who hadn't thought he had many fears, certainly none as harmless-looking as Star Brown. She turned reluctantly as he approached. She had the biggest brown eyes he'd ever seen. She wasn't afraid of him. Far from it. She was in charge here, tentative only about taking those watchful eyes off her mother. She looked like a small adult trying out an oversize chair.

He knelt beside her. "My name's Sam Beaudry. I'm Hilda's son. Your mother's a friend of mine." *Okay, not the most appealing introduction, but it was a start.*

"Hilda Beaudry is my grandmother."

Sam nodded. Now, how should he put this?

"Who's your daddy?"

"I don't have a daddy. I have Mom, and she has me." She turned from him, resuming her close watch. "She'll wake up pretty soon. Sometimes she sleeps for a long time, but she always wakes up."

He rubbed the twinge out of his left knee. "Has she been in the hospital like this before?"

"She said this is what would happen if I called nine-one-one. In school they told us to call nine-one-one if somebody was hurt or sick, but Mom said they might take her away if I did that." She eyed Sam suspiciously. "I didn't call anybody, but you came anyway."

"It's okay. Your mother made the call herself. She knew she needed a doctor, and now the doctor's trying to help her." He glanced up at the bed. From this angle

Merilee appeared to be even smaller, more childlike than her child. "I think she knows you're here."

"But she's asleep."

"Not exactly. She's resting, trying to get her strength back, but it's not the same as sleeping. One time when I was hurt, I was like this in a hospital, and I could kinda hear people around me."

"And you woke up?"

"Not right away. I'm just sayin' she might know we're here. So if there's something you want to tell her, she can probably hear you." His knee cracked as he rose for a better view of the patient's face. "Right, Merilee? It's Sam, in case you don't recognize the voice. I'm here with Star. We're hoping you'll open your eyes pretty soon, but we'll understand if you don't. We know you need your rest."

"Mommy?" Star leaned forward. "I don't know what to do, Mommy. I found the store, and I found my grandmother. Hilda Beaudry—I found her. Now what should I do?"

Sam shared with the child in the mother's silence. Life's breath came and went, came and went. How much effort Merilee put into the act was a mystery to Sam. She was hooked up to mechanical help, but maybe she was trying. He moved an armless chair from the corner of the room, set it at a right angle to Star's, straddled the seat and rested his forearms on the back, taking care not to block her view of her mother.

"You came a long way on the bus," he surmised. "How many days did it take?"

"Two, I think."

"Did your mom say how long she was planning to stay?"

"She said I might go to school here."

"Did she tell you anything about me?" he asked warily, and she glanced at him, equally cautious. "Her friend? Hilda's son, Sam?"

"I don't think so."

How far should he take this? "Do you have any relatives besides Hilda? Another grandma, maybe, or an auntie?"

"My other grandmother died. I never saw her." She eyed him briefly. "Are you like a cop or something?"

"I'm a sheriff. It's kind of like a cop, but I have to look after a whole county, and I have to get elected. I was a cop when I was in the marines. MP, they call it. Military police." Too far. Wrong direction. He could tell by her scowl.

"We don't really like cops."

"Oh." That hurt. "Who's *we?*"

"Well…" She glanced at her mother. Reminded she was on her own, she shrugged. "I mean, we like them when they help us. But I wouldn't call them up or anything. They can take anybody away. They might take bad people away, but they could take good people away, too. They might even take me away."

Damn. Where had that come from?

"Only if they thought somebody might be hurting you," he suggested.

"Even if they take a bad person away, he can come back," she confided, leaning closer to him in a way that made him feel better, like maybe he'd gained a little trust. "And when he comes back, he's twice as bad."

"Does the bad person have a name?"

"Maybe." She drew back. "Maybe not. It could be any bad person."

"I know how to handle bad people."

"Do you have a gun?" she whispered.

"I do. I killed a snake with it the other day." He gave a one-sided smile. "I have a jail, too. And handcuffs. A fast car with a big gold star painted on it. Bad people don't mess with me. Pretty soon we'll be gettin' the word out among the snakes."

"So, if I needed a cop, you'd be around? Because they're never around when you need one."

"You know Jim Whiteside?"

"Jimmy?"

Sam nodded. "Ask him. I'm *always* around. And Jim's *always* keeping an eye on me. I'm beginning to think he's on the county payroll, making sure I do my job. You ever need me, Jim knows right where to find me."

She wrinkled her little round nose. "He thinks he's a big smarty."

"He's a good kid, once you get to know him. It's good to have friends. You probably have a lot of friends in California." He tipped his head, inviting more confidence, hoping for names. "Maybe your mom has some friends there."

"We just moved again. We didn't know anybody in our new building." She stared at her mother, hoping. "Is she gonna wake up tomorrow?"

Sam knew if he couldn't say *yes* he was no help. He said nothing. He felt small and useless.

"Can't the doctor make her wake up?" Her voice was tiny and thin.

Ask me for something else, kid. An ice cream cone, a ride anywhere you want to go, a puppy, a Band-Aid. Anything but answers.

A tear plopped on her thumb.

He told himself to stay behind the back of the chair, use it as a shield, keep his distance. But before he knew it, he was standing, lifting the child into his arms and letting her hot tears drench the side of his neck.

No way could he ever cry. But he felt as though Star was doing it for him.

Chapter Four

It didn't matter to Maggie whether Sam had once loved Merilee Brown. It didn't matter to her whether he was the girl's father—unless he'd skipped out on them, which seemed unlikely, knowing Sam. But watching the three of them through the ICU glass gave rise to some soul-searching.

First, she shouldn't have been watching anything but monitors. Second, she was feeling an uncomfortable twinge in a bone she could have sworn she didn't have in her body—what self-respecting woman could be jealous of someone who was comatose—and, third, it did matter whether Sam was *still* in love with Merilee Brown. Because, first of all, the woman was probably dying. Second...

There was no *second*. Maggie was a nurse. Merilee

was a patient. Put the two together, end of search. Merilee's life was all that mattered at the moment.

Maggie dragged her attention back to the heart monitor. The *life* monitor. *Life was dear, and Death was jealous.*

"What's the—"

Hilda's voice gave Maggie a jolt.

"Sorry." Hilda joined her at the nurse's station, her gaze tagging after Maggie's lead. Through the window several feet away they watched Sam take a seat in the bedside chair with Star in his lap. He said something to her as he reached for the tissue box, and she nodded.

"Oh," Hilda whispered, and then, barely audibly, "Oh, Sam."

Maggie swallowed convulsively against a rising tide of tiny stingers.

Hilda touched Maggie's shoulder and leaned closer, as though she had a secret. "Lila said to tell you Jimmy wants to go home with her. I'm taking Star home with me as soon as she'll let me. That leaves you and Sam."

"For?"

"Coffee, maybe?"

"Hilda." Maggie warned her friend with a look. "He's not going to tell me anything he hasn't told you."

"Good." Hilda patted Maggie's shoulder. "Maybe you don't tell each other anything. Maybe you just look at each other and breathe easy over a cup of coffee."

What could it hurt?

"I'll ask."

She'd have to swallow some pride—first throat prickles, then pride—but given the circumstances, given the sweet moment between the big man and the little girl and the fact that Maggie had claimed a piece of it, maybe she could trade away a little pride. Give him one more chance. Forget that she'd invited Sam over for supper a couple of weeks ago, and he'd cancelled. Emergency, he'd said. Hell, Maggie's middle name was *Emergency*. The next move should have been his.

Not that she was making a move, but if she had any thought that there were moves to be made, the events of the day should have convinced her otherwise. Words like *issues, history* and *baggage* came to mind. Stuff she didn't need. She had no trouble handling herself professionally, and she was determined to start living the rest of her life with wits about her at all times. She'd almost decided she might be ready for an uncomplicated relationship with an uncomplicated man, and she'd been thinking about Sam Beaudry. A lot.

And now this.

So she asked, and he said *sure*—well, he'd nodded, anyway—and here they sat across from each other in Doherty's Café staring into their ceramic mugs as though the shape of a coffee oil slick might foretell the future. Maggie was determined to let the first word be Sam's. He could give her that much. She didn't care what the word was. Maybe he needed a friend or a confidante. Maybe he wanted her professional opinion.

Maybe he was watching some kind of reflection of the clock that was affixed to the wall behind him.

Okay, so she cared. She was a *nurse,* for heaven's sake.

"I think she's holding her own, Sam."

He glanced up. "Will they transfer her to Billings?"

"If there's something that can be done for her there that can't be done here, they'll consider moving her. But in her condition, it's a risky trip."

"Why?"

"As I said, she's holding her own. But she's frankly pretty frail. Most of her major organs are at risk of failing."

"Is it all from drugs?" he asked, and she glanced away. "What, you can't give out that kind of information?"

She offered an awkward smile. "I'm supposed to ask if you're a family member, and then I'm supposed to refer you to the doctor."

"What do you consider a family member?" He cast a searching glance at the ceiling before drilling her with a dark-eyed stare. "How about the son of the woman she says is her daughter's grandmother?"

"I…guess that works." Montana was different from Connecticut. Fewer people with more space between them added up to more slack. Indian country was definitely different, especially when it came to defining a family member, and most especially when children were involved. "We don't have all the test results. She has pneumonia. Probably hepatitis. She's on medication for diabetes. That's just for starters."

"Damn." He stared into his coffee for a moment. Then he drilled her again with those dark, straight-shooter eyes. "You think her daughter looks like me?"

Who but a man would ask such a self-centered question?

Who but a man would have to?

"She's a beautiful child."

"Yeah, I don't see it, either." He glanced away. "What did my mother tell you?"

"That she's never heard of Merilee Brown. That you used to tell her everything, but now you don't."

"I'd tell her if I had a kid." He bobbed a shoulder. "That I knew about."

"These things happen?"

"Not to me." He toyed with his spoon on the table. "We lived together for a while. I was crazy about her. I don't remember why."

"When you're crazy, nobody expects you to know why."

"Good point." Which he chalked up on an air board with the spoon. "I remember why I left."

"Being crazy wasn't working for you?"

He rewarded her cleverness with half a smile. "I would've danced to whatever tune she called, but I didn't have it in me. Couldn't learn the steps."

"Daddy don't rock 'n' roll?"

"I never took you for a smart-ass, Maggie." But he gave her the other half of the smile. "I could do that number. And I would."

She pressed her lips together, holding back on any remarks about Mama not dancing with him—maybe not even breathing much longer.

"Go ahead, say it."

She feigned innocence. "What?"

"Something like, 'Easy for you to say that now, Jack. How many years after you hit the road?'"

She laughed, less for the humor than for the surprise of it, coming from Sam. And the accuracy. "I won't tell you what I was thinking. Your guess is so much better." But close.

"I'm not much of a dancer, but I do a little mind reading sometimes."

"I see that." She sipped her coffee. "What's your next move?"

"I'm workin' on fortune-telling."

"I mean, being *the law in these parts,* what do you do now? You've got a comatose mother and a child who's—"

"Staying with her grandmother."

"We have a social worker."

"I know the drill, Maggie. I guarantee you I'm the only one in Bear Root, probably the only one in the whole state of Montana with any connection to Merilee Brown."

"Star's staying with her grandmother," Maggie echoed. *Which means...*

"While I sharpen up my detective skills. They haven't gotten much use lately."

"If I can help…" If she had a mirror in her purse, she could show him a clue. *Maybe that was what he was searching his pockets for.*

"We could be in serious trouble," he muttered as he gave up on his pants in favor of his shirt.

"That wasn't what I was thinking."

"No, I appreciate the offer." He smiled as he unbuttoned the flap on his left pocket—the one without the badge. "I thought I'd lost my billfold. They could've had the sheriff washing dishes here." He wagged a slim leather wallet. "Talk about crazy, huh?"

"Not me. Far be it for a smart-ass to talk about crazy."

"If I ask for help, it's the smart part I'll be lookin' for." He winked at her, a surprise that gave her butterflies. "I knew exactly what you were thinking."

* * *

Sam's apartment on the second floor of the old county building was hot, and not in a good way. There was no controlling the heat, no matter what the season.

He was never far away from his job, but he didn't mind. It was the way he'd lived most of his life. He'd grown up on the second floor of Allgood's Emporium. He'd billeted in camps, bunked in barracks, surfed a few couches, and he had to admit the sheriff's apartment wasn't half-bad as cramped, hot, on-site quarters went. He could always find some work to do when he couldn't sleep. He liked to keep close watch on any guests he was keeping in the four-cell county jail, which was right next door in the new courthouse building.

Some nights he'd drive around looking for trouble. Other times he'd dive into the never-ending stream of paperwork. On this night he went to the property cabinet and removed the Merilee Brown box.

He'd never known her to have much, but for a woman with a child, she had next to nothing. The personal possessions he'd removed from the motel room were remarkably scant. He had to believe she'd left home in a hurry, and he needed to find out why. An uncashed paycheck was his first clue. It was made out to Merilee with an unsigned endorsement to the order of Vic Randone. The check proved that Merilee was employed by the Gourmet Breakfast House in Long Beach until at least four weeks ago and that Randone was still taking money from her.

What the hell did she see in him?

Damn. Sam hadn't asked himself that question in a long time, and he wasn't going to let himself start in again. Back to the job at hand, he found a book about fairy-tale princesses and one about horses, a scrapbook full of baby pictures and growing girl pictures, drawings made with crayons, numbers and letters made by small hands and milestones described in a flowing hand. Sam knew Merilee's writing. It reminded him of the rise and fall of the ocean on a calm day at the beach.

Their early days—the three of them together—had been like that. Calm and sunny. They'd all found jobs—Merilee waiting tables, Vic and Sam driving trucks—and they'd made plans. Merilee would start out modeling—she had some experience—which would lead to commercials, which would lead to bigger things. Vic would manage her—he had no experience—and Sam would keep the rent paid and the cupboards from going bare. Sam had done his part. His was the easy part, according to his roommates.

Easy, as long as he looked the other way.

Easy, until there *was* no other way and he couldn't stomach it anymore.

But the child in the picture was easy on his eyes. He could see her mother in her—the shape of her mouth, ears, chin—but she was her own little person. And he might be her father. There was an outside chance.

High and outside. How many strikes did that make? Well, he knew one thing. She'd found her way to Bear Root, where, father or no father, Sam would protect her. Merilee must have known that. She'd left home in a hurry, and she'd come to his hometown. If he hadn't been there, somebody would have been able to find him. She must have known that, too. Unlike Merilee, Sam had family.

What else had she considered important enough to bring with her?

A few clothes for the child—which he'd delivered earlier—and fewer for herself. There was a zippered bag containing small bottles of toiletries and some sweet-smelling leakage, a couple of magazines, two bracelets, a ring and a religious medallion on a gold chain inside a plastic soap box. He'd never known Merilee to be religious. The absence of leads—an address book, mail, lists, notes, some kind of electronic device—was frustrating. The fact that Randone was the only name to be found was worse than frustrating. It was a flying scream and a flashing light.

Vic was a wild man. He was the kind of guy who always knew how to jump-start a party, how to double down and ratchet up. When it was just the two of them knocking around together, no problem. Sooner or later Vic would flame out, and Sam could always drive. No matter what direction they'd taken, Sam could always find the way back to home base. Then along came Merilee, and Sam had been set to let Vic find his own way, which he did. But he took Merilee with him. And the two of *them* together, *big* problem. Randone was a wild man, and Merilee was wild for Randone.

Sam rubbed his thumb over the medallion, wondered about the serene female image and what it meant to its owner. Somewhere along the line maybe Merilee had found religion. Or maybe she'd found the medallion. Or maybe…

Maybe he'd go for a walk and clear his head, prepare to take a swing at the next pitch. The right pitch this time. He pictured Maggie sitting across the table from him, being easy on him and up-front with him at the same time. She had a nice way about her.

Good eye, Sam. Good eye.

He knew one more thing. He could play ball. He was a good sport, a reliable defender and an unfailing shooter—assets that had served him in fields where lives were on the line instead of games. He'd learned to be patient, particular and sure. He was not—nor would he ever be—a wild man.

Lila and Jimmy were both asleep when Maggie got home. She sat down on the side of her son's small bed, smoothed her favorite fan-shaped cowlick and pulled his blanket up to his chin in defense against the mountain air, so fresh and healthful, so chilly after sunset, but one of the changes she cherished most in her new home. Even after two years it still seemed new.

Jimmy threw the blanket off and turned from back to side, his hand homing in on her forearm, which he rubbed in his sleep the way he had when he was a toddler. His little-boy moments were fewer and more precious all the time, and she regretted any she might be missing. Or worse, taking for granted. There were times when she regretted not having her own place—times when Jimmy seemed just as happy to be with Lila as he was with Maggie. Ah, but those were her small-mind, small-heart moments. Lila Demery was a blessing in their lives.

When Maggie had come across an online plea for nurses in isolated Western communities and applied pretty much on impulse, she didn't realize that housing was limited in communities like Bear Root. The town was half incorporated, half Indian reservation, and all tucked between a mountain and a foothill and surrounded by all kinds of federally protected turf. Houses like the two-story Victorian she shared with Lila, a social worker, were rare. The house had been in Lila's family for three generations, and it had a big backyard with the view of snow-capped peaks that she'd left home for. Maggie and Jimmy had separate bedrooms and bathrooms upstairs, while Lila occupied the master suite on the main floor. Okay, *suite* was pushing it. The only bathtub was upstairs, but Lila had determined the room assignments. Yes, indeed, Lila was a blessing.

Maggie was programming the pot for morning coffee when she heard the knock at the door. It was late, and she was tired, but she had to remember she wasn't in Connecticut anymore. Out West people helped each other, no question. You never knew when it might be your turn, and you wouldn't want the only help for miles around to be somebody whose troubles you'd ignored. So she padded to the door in her scuffs, turned the porch light on and peeked through the window in the door.

Sam?

He stood with his back to her, but she knew him by the impossible length of his back and breadth of his shoulders and the way he stood with legs shoulder-width apart, one hand tucked against the small of his back. Parade rest, or very close to it. Any true military brat like Maggie would recognize the stance, if not the man.

But she recognized the man. She'd admired him from this angle before, watched him when he didn't know it. She'd hoped he didn't. He didn't seem like the kind of man who would take advantage, but seeming and being were worlds apart. She'd learned the hard way, and now she had a child to consider.

By now he surely knew she was watching him. He allowed her the time. In spite of the light, he waited until the door opened before making his about-face. He nodded, unsmiling, as though she'd sent for him and the book he carried against his thigh.

She smiled wordlessly. *Like it or not, Sam, it's your move.*

"I was on my way over to my mother's place."

Maggie kept right on smiling.

"I saw your light on." He nodded again, this time toward the picture window. "Living room light, I thought maybe you were still…" At long last he cracked a smile. "I don't know about you, but I drank too much coffee."

"Come on in." She backed the door open wider.

"It's nice out." He didn't move. "You feel like walking?"

"Jimmy's asleep." She glanced across the living room toward the hallway and the light under the bedroom door. "But Lila's here. I'll let her know where I'm going." She paused midmove. "Where am I going?"

"With me."

"To Hilda's?"

"I started out for there, but she's not expecting me. This is better."

"A rare change of heart?"

"Direction." He opened the storm door and stepped inside. "I change direction all the time. It's my business.

You follow the leads, they take you in all directions." He handed her the book. "Found this photo album in Merilee's stuff. Pictures of the little girl from when she was a baby."

"Sam." She spared him an indulgent smile as she paged through the album. "Her name is Star."

"I was thinkin' I'd take it over there and see what she might say about them."

"Star?"

"Star. No middle name on her birth certificate, just Star Brown. Like she fell out of the sky and—" he slapped his palm with the back of his other hand "—hit the ground runnin'."

"She had a long road ahead of her, L.A. to Bear Root."

"Yeah." He jerked his chin toward her feet. "You got some better shoes?"

She looked down. She'd gotten as far as getting out of her shoes but she hadn't shed the uniform yet, and neither had he. She chuckled as she kicked off the pink scuffs. Off duty, going for a walk, and still in uniform. Both of them, how sad. If being married to the job was a major commonality between them, these butterflies he kept giving her should probably be set free while they could still fly.

Sam carried the album under his arm like a schoolboy walking his girl home. But it was past Bear Root's ten o'clock school-night curfew. The town had gone to bed, the air was cool and still and the sky ran riot with stars. Maggie drank it in—Rocky Mountain Elixir— and enjoyed Sam's story about catching her son peeking in his window. She told him Jimmy's wild tale about Sam getting the drop on a pair of cattle rustlers, and he told her that it was all true.

Then, out of the clear blue he asked, "You think she's here for good?"

Maggie's heart fell. "You mean…"

"Star."

She shrugged. "Unless you can come up with some closer kin, I think they both might be." But she couldn't say they'd be sharing the same digs, so to speak.

Sam fell quiet. When they reached Main, they started to turn in opposite directions.

"The Emporium is this way," she said.

"My place is this way. I want to drop this off." The metallic trim on the album glinted under the corner streetlamp. "And Star's probably asleep."

"That wasn't so hard, was it? Star is a very pretty name. It evokes—"

"I want you to take a look at the rest of their stuff. See if you can help me figure out what's goin' on. I mean, you're a woman, a mother, a good—"

"No." Maggie shook her head, took a step back. "I don't want to look at Merilee's *stuff*, Sam. I don't want to talk about it. I don't want to think about it. I'm off duty."

"It's not like that." He closed in, claiming her space. "Maggie, it's not like that."

"What isn't like *what?"* He was too big, and she was too easy. *Been there, done that, got the hard knocks diploma.* The hand she put between them was a warning as well as a space maker. "I wasn't expecting you, either. Call me next time."

She turned to backtrack, and he followed.

She stopped. "What are you doing?"

"Walking you back."

"I'll be fine."

She would be angry—first with him, and then with herself—but she would be fine after that because she would not be hung up on a man who was hung up on another woman. Never again, she promised herself. *Again*.

She was on the move, but he still had her back.

"What the hell did I do?" His sigh softened his tone. "I'm no better at this than I ever was."

"I'd say you've got that right, but I'd only be guessing." And guessing meant looking back. *She was not looking back*.

"Maggie, wait."

He turned her to him, eye-to-eye, face-to-face. He had her at *Maggie*. He had her looking back, looking up, looking for more than just a clue to what he wanted. Maggie, what? Wait for *what*?

For the source of the heat in his dark eyes. She was transfixed. He slid his hand over her shoulder to her nape, his warm fingers making her skin tingly, her head light, her body unable to move. His other arm came around her for purchase, the edge of the book braced on her hip, as he drew her to him—belly-to-belly, thighs-to-thighs, mouth-to-mouth, tongue-to-tongue— and made her feel drunk. Drink, drink, drink, he drank her, and oh, how good it felt to be drunk and drunk, drawn in and gulped and gulped as though he, dying of thirst, found her fatally delicious.

"It's like that," he whispered. "For me right now, right here, it's like that."

She gripped handfuls of his jacket—the tapered part where it hugged his long back and slender waist—and looked up at him. It was a curious moment. Her heart thudded erratically, and her brain entertained images of the two of them together in mouth-watering, mind-numbing ways. She knew those ways. She knew what it could be like. She stepped back, losing touch and finding thought.

He tried to take her space back. She held him off.

"You can't come home with me, Sam. For me, right now, it's like that."

Chapter Five

Maggie stood quietly with Merilee's five mourners, but her unfortunate prediction echoed loudly in her head. Merilee was here for good. Her remains would remain, rooted now and forever in Bear Root. *Here for good*. Dumb statement, *dumb*. Which was what she should have been—dumb as in *mum*. Nurses did not diagnose, and they were not supposed to prognosticate or prophesy.

She couldn't claim she hadn't meant it the way it sounded, either. Not that she was claiming anything aloud, but she didn't have to. She was her own worst critic, her own judge, her own scorekeeper. From the time they'd spent alone together in the ambulance, Maggie had known the score. Merilee had come to Bear Root to die, and there was no kind of care, intensive or otherwise, that could have made a difference. Diabetes, hepatitis, pneumonia, addiction—in Merilee's case, a fatal combination. No sooner had she been admitted to the hospital than her organs had begun to fail, one after another in quick succession. She had not regained consciousness. She had foiled the decision to transfer her person by becoming a body.

The graveside service was brief, but Maggie had not attended a sadder one. The only crying came from a hawk wheeling overhead before riding the air current toward the nearest mountain peak, that much closer to heaven. The two people who'd actually known the dead woman were barely present. Dazed and dry-eyed, Star allowed Hilda to stand with her and hold her hand. Maggie imagined Hilda letting go and Star drifting up, up, and away. Sam, too, set himself apart. Pressed and polished as always, he seemed untouched and untouchable. On the heels of the pastor's final prayer, Maggie uttered the only *amen*. The rising hawk cried out again, and then greeted its own echo.

Star spoke to Hilda, and Hilda said a few quiet words to Sam, who lifted the girl so she could lay a clutch of purple irises and yellow tulips on her mother's casket. The colors—chosen, she said, because they were Merilee's favorites—also blanketed the nearby hill slope in a riot of spring wildflowers. Star had actually smiled when they'd arrived, calling attention to the match she'd made.

She clung to Hilda as they followed the pastor away from the grave. Sam walked beside his mother, and Maggie brought up the rear. She was touched by the way Hilda had taken to her role as though she'd been part of the little girl's life from the start. They had been together only a few days, but they had become inseparable. Merilee had chosen not to die with her child in the room—Maggie had seen enough death to know that there was a choice made from one instant to the next, the holding on to the letting go—just as surely she had chosen the woman who would see her child through the loss. She had known the woman only by her son, and on that basis had she made her last move.

Right. And Jimmy would someday get elected president on the basis of his I-owe-it-all-to-my-mother stump speech.

Rub the stardust out of your eyes, Maggie. This is a tragedy, and there is nothing remotely romantic about it.

As they neared the four vehicles parked along the dirt road that surrounded the windswept graveyard, Star looked up at Hilda and said, "I want to go to school now."

"We'll get you enrolled tomorrow." Hilda smoothed a wisp of hair back from her temple and tucked it behind her ear. "First thing."

"Jimmy's at school right now. It's a school day, and I should be in school, too."

"Right now?"

"Kids have to go to school. If they don't, they get taken away. That's the law." She turned to Sam, who walked hat in hand, seemingly lost in his thoughts. But he met Star's gaze as though she'd called his name. "Isn't it?" she demanded. "Don't you have a law about kids being in school?"

"Kids…yeah, they have to go to school unless their parents…" He glanced at Hilda and Maggie by turns, then back to Star. "But you're okay. Nobody's getting arrested today."

"I can sign myself up," she said, bringing the procession to a standstill. She looked up to face the man down. "I have my birth certificate and everything."

"How about your shots?" Sam asked offhandedly as he put his hat on.

Maggie shot him a volley of daggers—was he trying to be funny?

But Star beat her to the verbal punch. "I've had all my shots, but I'll take 'em over again if you don't believe me."

Sam looked at the child as though she'd knocked the wind out of him. He didn't look for any help from the women. He wouldn't get any, and Star didn't need any. Maggie smiled to herself as she watched it dawn on him—the hint of a smile, first in his eyes, then at the corner of his mouth—that little Star had him cold.

"I believe you," he said solemnly. "And I'll back you. Right now. Today." He offered his hand. "I'll take you to school myself."

She eyed the brown-and-tan patrol car with Bear Root County Sheriff emblazoned on the side. "They might think I *did* get arrested."

"They might think you're the kind of star that gets an official escort." His hand didn't waver. "You comin'?"

She stepped away from Hilda's side, hesitated, took another step and put her small hand into Sam's, which swallowed hers up. Without another word they got into the sheriff's car and drove away.

Hilda liked being a grandmother, but she loved— *loved*—having a little girl to fuss over. It was every bit as much fun as she'd thought it would be, back when shopping for school clothes meant T-shirts in primary colors and jeans in blue, or when there could be no frills or pink parts on the birthday presents, or when she who hated any game involving a ball was consigned to shagging pop flies for Zach because Sam was determined to get his younger brother into Little League before he was technically old enough.

Within the first week of grandmother-hood, Hilda had rediscovered pastel colors, ankle socks and Barbie dolls. It took some practice to perfect the ponytail and some persuasion to be permitted to add a ribbon. But it all paid off in the mirror with Star's bright-eyed approval reflected in the foreground, backed by Hilda's satisfaction. They were becoming a team without throwing or catching anything but 'atta girls.

And they suddenly had fans. Regular noncustomer company without so much as a meeting scheduled or a supper planned. Hilda wasn't sure which came first, Sam checking in every day, or Jimmy walking Star home from school on the excuse that Maggie needed something from the Emporium. Either way regularly brought Maggie into the mix, sometimes on the phone, almost as often in person. And the mix seemed to gel naturally. It felt like an expanded family in the making.

Lucky laid claim to Star by curling up on the foot of her bed in "the boys' room" as though it was where he always slept. Hilda might have felt slighted, but Star had chosen Sam's boyhood bed—a sign, surely—creating a picture worthy of one of her fondest dreams: little sleepyhead tucked into little twin bed shared with little, black-and-white three-legged dog, ambient night-lighting courtesy of an old plastic palomino plugged in near the base of the wall.

Perfection.

A new week ushered in a few changes in the routine at Allgood's Emporium. Sam suddenly had more time for meals with Ma, and Maggie started taking the Beaudrys at their word when they said Jimmy was "no trouble." Within the week, five places were staked out at Hilda's table. Within a scant two weeks, a face was missed when a chair was empty. Was Maggie working tonight? Had Sam brought in a new hoosegow occupant? Hilda had gone from eating at the counter with Lucky at her feet to presiding over a table again. And she liked it.

"I remembered to take your birth certificate into the school today," Sam told Star over the strawberry shortcake Maggie had made—or, at least, assembled. "Proved to them that you're really seven."

"And a half."

"That half is important. They said, 'Seven *and a half.* That makes a little more sense.' They thought you were the typical woman, lying about your age."

Hilda jabbed him in the shoulder with a slightly arthritic finger. "You watch how you talk, young man, badge or no badge."

"I'm sorry, Ma. Fibbing." He tipped his head in deference to Star. "They thought you were a very small twelve-year-old."

"Fib, schmib," Hilda grumbled. "You be careful how you use that word *typical* around here."

"Hell, I just got reelected. I can talk straight now for another year and a half." He winked at Star. "I'm just sayin', that half is important."

"Do I have to get more shots?"

"I wouldn't know about that. What do you think, Maggie?"

"We've searched online for the name of Star's old school and gotten the address. I don't know about the legal hoops, but that's a place to start."

"You could maybe give Star those shots personally, huh, Maggie? She gave me a big ol' tetanus shot once. Didn't even hurt. She gives good shots."

"Only on doctor's orders." Maggie signaled Sam with the coffeepot, and he nodded for a refill. "You and Lila can get it all worked out with the school, and I'll be ready to step up to the plate." She smiled at Star. "If needed."

"With her pointy little bat." Jimmy flashed a devilish grin as he jabbed a strawberry with his fork.

"It won't bother me," Star assured him. "I'm not the one who fell off Jaws and cried like a baby."

Jimmy tucked his bandaged elbow close to his side. The heated look he gave Star said, *No fair.* But no one backed him up since he'd been the one to tell Star that she had to ride double with Sam and he got to have a horse to himself because *she* was only seven. He'd forgotten about that half.

After the table was cleared, Sam brought out a green-and-pink scrapbook, which he lovingly placed on the table. "I brought this over," he told Star, his voice as gentle as a lullaby. "I thought you might be ready to look at it with me. Maybe you could tell me about the pictures."

She hung back. "Tell you what?"

He glanced at Hilda. She knew that mother-may-I? look, and she gave him the subtle yes-you-may nod.

Sam was her good son, her gentle son, the one any female worth her God-given intuition would know she could count on.

Okay, maybe Hilda was thinking a little defensively lately, and it wasn't Star who had her thinking that way. It was a poor, sad, dead woman.

Shame on you, Hilda Beaudry.

"What's goin' on in the pictures, how old you were, stuff like that." Sam patted his denim-clad thigh, inviting Star to take a seat.

"My mom says it's my legacy." She chose a chair. "Did you already look?"

"I did. But Maggie and Hilda haven't seen them. They love baby pictures."

"You show us yours, and I'll show you his," Hilda said. Sam groaned.

"I'm taking Lucky outside," Jimmy said, sounding slightly disgusted.

"I'm right behind you, Jim."

Star's small hand stayed Sam's much bigger one on the table as she challenged him with a look. "I thought you wanted to see my pictures."

"Well, we do," he said, and Hilda and Maggie chimed in unison, "We *do*."

"We don't." Jimmy bounced a tennis ball in his palm, Lucky barked and they were out the door and charging down the second-story back steps.

Sam patted his thigh again, inviting Star to "Make room for the rest of the audience."

Star obliged, stiff and hesitant at first, and Sam was, too, even though he was working hard not to let it show. They weren't used to each other yet. *Give them time,*

Hilda told herself as she watched the pages go by. Only one face in the pictures interested her. Baby Star taking a bath in the kitchen sink. Toddler Star pushing her empty stroller. Birthday-party Star blowing out three candles. Sam was angling for details, but putting names to the faces of strangers didn't interest Hilda. She saw her granddaughter growing up.

The images she'd promised to show off flashed through her mind—baby Sam with his handsome young father, who'd died of a heart attack when Sam was fourteen. Sam taking his first steps into Tom Beaudry's outstretched arms. Sam at age three welcoming baby brother Zach to Allgood's Emporium. Hilda saw the resemblance between Star and Sam, even if no one else noticed. A mother…a *grand*mother knew these things.

"You forgot this guy," Sam said, pointing to a dark-haired man in dark glasses standing beside Star on a rocky beach and smiling for the camera. Squinting against the sun, arms folded tightly around her jacket, the wind lifting her long hair away from her face, she looked small, separate and serious beyond her years.

"That's Vic," she said, deadpan.

"Vic?"

Notice, Hilda telepathed to her son, *she doesn't say Daddy.*

But she did say, "Vic Randone."

"I thought I recognized him." Sam tapped the face in the picture with his forefinger. "I knew him, back when I knew your mother. But he had more hair then."

"Did you like him?" Star wanted to know.

Sam glanced at her. "Did you?"

"No. I don't know why she put that picture back in

here." She turned the page forcefully and pointed to a stocky black woman with gray hair. "This is Mrs. Carey. She lived down the hall from us, but she moved away after Christmas. She was our friend."

"When was the last time you saw Vic?" Sam asked.

"I don't know."

"Was it just before you left on the bus? Or was it a long while before that? Did he ever…"

Hilda laid her hand on Sam's free thigh and gave him a warning glance as she drew attention to the facing page. "Where are you in this picture? That looks like fun."

"Oceanside Park." Star's tone moved up in scale. "Those are bumper cars. You crash into each other, but you don't get hurt because the cars have bouncy—"

"Who took the picture?" Sam wondered. Star scowled. "It's you and your mom in the car. I just wondered who—"

"I don't wanna talk about him now," she said quietly. "Don't ask me about him, okay?"

"Okay."

"That's why Grandma looked at you so hard. Don't you know that?"

"He would if he wasn't a *typical* man," Hilda said, smiling with the thrill of being referred to for the first time as *Grandma*. Not Hilda. Not *my grandmother*. She was, at last, Grandma.

"Okay, truce." Sam chuckled as he closed the album. "Where's Jim? I'm badly outnumbered here."

"And for once I'm not," Hilda said. "I kinda like it. You gotta understand about Sam, honey, he's a cop." She reached out to Star, who slid from Sam's lap into Hilda's hands. "*Sheriff*. Closest thing we have up here in Bear Root. Sam was always a quiet boy, a good boy, minded his own business, never asked too many questions, and then he got bit by the law enforcement bug, and he doesn't know when to quit. But you don't have to worry about Sam. He's still a good—"

"I'm not worried." Star turned back to Sam. "We didn't tell him where we were going. He doesn't know."

Sam nodded.

"Jimmy says you know how to shoot a gun and you have a jail and handcuffs and you can lock people up."

"When they break the law," Sam said. "I try to protect people from getting hurt. I'll protect you from…" He cut a pointed glance at the photo album.

"I wish you coulda protected my mom."

"So do I."

"You know what else Jimmy says?" Hilda pushed her chair away from the table and Sam's investigation and pictures of Star's old life. With a quick turn of her head and an eager glance, Star betrayed her interest in whatever Jimmy had to say. "He says he loaned you a baseball mitt and you proved to have a good arm."

"For a girl," Star amended.

"Oh, honey, ignore that part. You gotta understand about Jimmy, too. He's a boy. They have to add that on. Kind of like when somebody sneezes and you say *gesundheit.* It's male superstition." Hilda offered Star her hand. "Let's go downstairs and look in the storeroom for the Beaudry baseball box. You've got baseball in your blood, girl."

"I do?"

"Of course you do." Hilda laughed off Sam's hooded scowl. "Who's your grandma?"

* * *

Maggie pretended to ignore Sam while she tidied up around the stove and sink. There was really nothing left to tidy, and she was keenly aware every time Sam turned another scrapbook page. His daughter—*his daughter?*—Hilda's granddaughter had made a wish, and he'd echoed it. Now he was counting regrets. And Maggie should have been outside playing baseball rather than hanging back out of…what? Curiosity? Sympathy? Some fragile, springtime-budding wish of her own?

Friendship. Pure, simple, honest friendship. She could really go for a good friendship right about now, especially with a man like Sam Beaudry. He was…

He looked up from the pictures directly into her eyes, slowly closing the book. No smile. No comment.

Damn, he was reading her mind again.

Sam was probably quite pure and honest, but simple? Uh-uh. He was big and beautiful and suddenly quite complicated, at least from Maggie's perspective. He had no idea how needy he was at this moment. He thought he did. She could see it in his eyes. *I need a few minutes up real close and extremely personal with you, woman. Pure, simple, honest sex. Need met, problem solved.* But Maggie knew better. He could steal her heart without trying, maybe without even knowing. But his need would not go away with the theft *accompli,* and it would still be just as complicated.

He stood, his dark eyes never wavering. She couldn't resist them, and she knew she was giving herself away.

"You don't wanna play ball?"

"Not…right now."

"Good." He nodded toward the back door and the voices floating up from the yard and through the kitchen window. Dear, sweet, happy voices. "Let's sit outside and watch Ma bridge the gender gap."

She felt a little dizzy, as though she'd crept close to the edge of a steep drop and looked down. She felt silly, too. If he'd read her mind, he had to be laughing on the inside. Payback for the night he'd kissed her and she'd walked away.

She laughed on the outside. On the inside she was hanging on to the rail.

The back door opened onto a deck that was clearly a relatively recent addition to the old structure. It had yet to be used this season—Sam had to pull off the tarp he'd tied over the glider last fall—but its east-facing orientation provided evening shade and a view of the rocky, rolling hills, spring green grass amid red bluffs and granite outcroppings.

"The best seats in the house." The glider put up a rusty squawk as Maggie settled in. "You can see the whole east side of town."

"All four paved streets."

"And the rising sun."

"Fire in the sky. This started out as a fire escape." Lucky barked at him as he peered over the rail and exchanged a quick thumbs-up with Jimmy. "Then Dad built a small landing with an awning," he continued, joining Maggie on the two-passenger seat. "He liked to sit up here in the summer and watch the ball games. He usually caught the last few innings after he closed the store. The deal was that Ma got to go to the games as long as she opened up in the morning when he liked to sleep in. After he died, I fixed this up for her, made it big enough so she could bring her friends out here. She calls it her veranda."

"It's warm enough to start meeting out here for book club again." Maggie loved Hilda's book club. The women met in a back corner of the store most of the time, but when the weather permitted, Hilda loved to show off her "veranda."

The club had helped Maggie make a name for herself in Bear Root other than *that new nurse.* Thanks to Hilda, who'd warned that if she didn't get into something outside the hospital, she'd still be *that new nurse* when she moved on, which most new people did. Or so Maggie had been told a time or ten. And, indeed, for a while there had only been one thing besides her job keeping Maggie in Bear Root, and she was looking at it.

"This is a gorgeous view."

"You won't find much better. I don't know what I was lookin' for, but I sure tried. Part of the reason Ma hardly ever goes anywhere, I guess. That and the fact that she's like you. Dedicated. She doesn't like to close the store or leave it with anyone else for very long. It belonged to her father, who took it over from his father."

"Is Allgood her maiden name?"

"We carry *all goods.*" His eyes twinkled with the repetition of the answer he'd probably heard many times. "Her name was McKenzie."

"And your dad was Native-American."

"Chippewa and French, heavy on the Chippewa. It's called Métis. Mixed-blood. Mom's people came from Canada before Dad's, but she's mostly Scot, a little Cree. Trader blood."

"Star looks a lot like—" She glanced away. She'd spoken without thinking, and she was about to presume even more. "I can see the resemblance, Sam."

"I wish I could." He shrugged, gave her a tight, apologetic smile.

"Are you willing?"

"Yeah. *Sure.*" He sighed. "I don't know. Maybe I don't know how, what to look for." A sardonic chuckle gave way to a frown as he turned to her. "Kind of a woman thing, isn't it? You ever hear a man say, 'That baby looks just like you'?"

"Now that you mention it…" She touched his bare arm, smiling to herself as she tried to remember when she'd last seen him out of his "sheriff shirt." Smiling over Hilda's and Jimmy's cheers for Star over some play she'd made below the view from the deck. Smiling over Sam's faded Red Sox T-shirt, recalling the time she'd finally gotten more than a few words out of him when they'd discovered a common loyalty to the team. She'd surprised herself by playing her interest way out of proportion. But she did own a Red Sox cap, and she smiled over that. And how cute he'd looked when Jimmy had— with her blessing—presented it to him.

"You're worried about this Randone," she said.

"You see any resemblance there?"

"None."

"You might if you met him in person. They say looks can be deceiving. Well, there's not much about Vic that *isn't* deceiving."

"Are you worried that you're not Star's father? Or scared that you are?"

"Worrying is a waste of time and energy. Doesn't change anything or solve anything." He slid his hand over hers. "So don't try to get me started."

"I'm no fan of worrying. I didn't mean to…"

"I know. You didn't mean to think out loud." He gave her hand a quick little squeeze. "I don't mind. You say what you're thinking. It means we're friends."

"Good." She gave one solid nod. "Friends."

"Good. Friends." He lifted one corner of his mouth, eyes twinkling. "You tryin' out for Hollywood Indian?"

She laughed.

"Hey, when I was out in L.A. they offered me a part in a movie."

"Really?"

"Yeah, really. I went with Merilee for one of her tryouts. I was just hangin' out. Some woman said I had the look they wanted, and did I have some kinda union card, and could I read. She meant *would* I read, 'cause the part had lines, but I took it like she didn't think I could read." He lifted one shoulder. "Okay, I purposely took it like that, but what the hell. Merilee was steamed at me for at least a week. I don't know if it was because they wanted me to read when she was the one lookin' to try out, or because I had a little fun puttin' the woman on." He chuckled. "Acted like a big, dumb Hollywood Indian."

"And she was looking for an actor."

"Lookin' for a big, dumb Hollywood Indian, I guess. Said she'd help me get the damn union card." He gave her a you-believe-that? look and shook his head. "I embarrassed Merilee, and I don't ever do that, not purposely. That was about the time I realized I was losin' it. Self-respect, mainly. Started thinking about enlisting." He came back from the memory and noticed her anew. "Cold?"

The word made her shiver, and she laughed. "A little bit, now that the sun's…"

He lifted his arm around her shoulders and tucked her in close. "Still friends?"

"Good friends." She relaxed, muscle by muscle.

"Then tell me something about your people."

"My father was a navy pilot. My mother's a nurse. I was an only child. Half-Texan, half-New Yorker. I don't know about blood, but they spoke different languages. And I have no roots."

He gave her a quick, warm squeeze. "Where are they now?"

"Arlington National Cemetery and Cameroon. My father was killed in an accident. He survived Vietnam and went down in a light plane during a storm. My mother joined the Peace Corps after I finished school. She never remarried. Very independent woman, my mother."

"I see the resemblance," he said with a smile in his voice.

"No, she's…" Maggie took a moment, a breath, made herself comfortable with the power and glory that was Mother, and then said what she always said, what she knew for sure. "My mother is fearless and tireless, dedicated and…and good. She's very good at what she does, and she's just a very good person. She's been in Africa since…"

"You worry about her?"

"Now, wouldn't that be a waste of time and energy?" It felt good to laugh in the face of the short-comings she rarely thought about anymore unless she was stacking them up against Mother's high hopes. "I miss her. I might have followed her if…well, if things had been different. I was never married to Jimmy's father. It was never a consideration. Not for either of us."

Maggie stared hard at the empty ball field beyond the Emporium's backyard. She sensed Sam's empathy, felt his almost imperceptible nod.

And she was encouraged.

"I had it all planned out, back when I was young and innocent. All my bases would be covered. First school, then travel and adventure, then love, marriage, baby carriage. Beyond that, it's kind of hazy, but you're young and innocent, and all you know is that you know it all." She looked up at Sam and smiled. "Life's full of surprises, isn't it? Things you never dreamed."

"What would you change?"

"Nothing." She raised her eyebrows. "The numbers on my last lottery ticket." Eyebrows drew in on that one. "No, not even that. Change one thing you've already done, pull one thread, and it could unravel everything."

"What about the mistakes?"

"You mean the hard lessons? They're part of getting from young and innocent to older and wiser. I know I'm older than you."

"Not by much," he said dismissively.

"And I'm wiser than I used to be. So are you. Not everyone can say that, and when they can't, it shows." She gave a tight smile. "So what would you change?"

"I'd'a said *nothing* a couple of weeks ago. Now, I

don't know. I feel like I went AWOL, you know? Took the easy way out."

"Well, my friend, you're not out anymore."

He shook his head and glanced away. "I've never been this scared in my life, and I don't even know what I'm scared of."

"Take it easy, Sam." She laid her hand over the one that warmed her shoulder. "You deal with surprises every day. You have good instincts. You have all the—"

His kiss consumed her like a summer wind, stirring every part of her. She reached for him, one arm around his neck, one trapped between them. She heard him catch his breath as she grabbed a wad of soft T-shirt and pressed her fist against his hard chest. His kiss turned gentle, his full lips petitioning hers in small ways for an opening and a welcoming and an in-kind reply. But she wanted him wanting her, and for that she pressed closer even as she tipped her head to the side—away but not far—and traced the curve of his ear with her thumb. A pleasured sound escaped her throat, and she felt the shape of his mouth widen against the corner of hers.

"Was that a surprise?" he whispered.

She nodded, but before he could go from smile to laugh, she claimed the upper hand with a turnabout kiss. And she was pretty sure she took his breath away.

Chapter Six

"I come bearing crackers, cheese and children," Maggie called out as she batted the beaded bell pull cross-stitched with the invitation *Give Me A Jingle*.

The Emporium's cheerful bell was more greeting than demand for service.

When the door was open, Allgood's proprietor was always within earshot, and the tinkling bell simply said *Hi-ho Hilda!*

"Can I ring it?" Jimmy pleaded.

"Once is enough." Star's sharp glance accused him of insufferable immaturity. "We're going right back outside as soon as I get the Frisbee."

"Good plan. I'll remember next time, Jimmy." Maggie raised her voice above the ceiling fan's lazy *whap-whap*. "Lila has to work late, so she probably won't make it." She peered around a candy end cap.

"But I saw Jerry at the clinic waiting for an appointment. She had the book with her, and she was bookmarking pages, so you know she'll be here with all kinds of commentary."

"I had a call from Minnie." The voice came from the corner still fondly tagged the Dugout, even though Hilda had, with mostly female encouragement, replaced the motley collection of sports memorabilia and dust-collecting taxidermy with locally handcrafted items that were for sale and a friendship quilt that was not. "She'll be here if nothing comes of any of the disasters she's waitin' on. Which means she'll be here."

"I'm sorry." What seemed like a perfectly acceptable contribution when she'd bagged it up looked negligible now that Maggie saw the spread laid out on the card table Hilda had set up near the cold woodstove. Veggies and dip, tea sandwiches, Hilda's mouth-watering Rhu Bars. "I was going to bake something."

"This is fine, honey." Hilda set the brown bag aside, and Maggie knew it would still be there for her to take back home with her when the meeting was over. *Oh, well. She'd tried.*

Hilda glanced behind Maggie. "What happened to the kids?"

"Star and Lucky met us on the corner. She's going to show Jimmy and Lucky new skills with the Frisbee."

As if to prove their presence, two voices and a bark wafted through the open window overlooking the backyard. Maggie moved the café curtain aside just as Lucky sprang like a bottle rocket and snatched the green plastic disk out of the air.

"I never could throw one of those things. Star picked

it up right away. Her da—" Hilda gave a diffident smile. "Sam showed her how."

Maggie raised her brow. "Is it for sure?"

"We've filed with the Tribal court and the county, both. And we have Lila's backing, so we shouldn't have any problem getting temporary custody." Hilda fanned a small stack of yellow paper napkins on the counter next to the coffee that was always on at Allgood's and the tea that was a book club exclusive. "Sam's doing his job, of course. You know Sam—no stone left unturned, even if he's only lookin' for trouble.

"He found out Merilee's mother is dead and her father left a long time ago. So far, so good. Or…not so good, maybe, but simple. I'd love for the court, the county, whoever has the power, to just put Star on the fast track, get her over this rough patch, through the system and into Sam's custody permanently. If we had something in writing from the mother it would be a slam dunk. It's what she wanted, no doubt about that."

"He could get paternity testing."

"I don't know, he seems…" Hilda waved her doubts away. "Lila says he doesn't have to unless there's a challenge from somebody."

"That's true. Back home we had a neighbor win custody and eventually adopt a child whose single mother went off the deep end. No relation, but the neighbor was a friend of the mother's, and the child was over there all the time. It was in the child's best interest, which was otherwise in short supply. So, if that's what Sam wants…"

"I'm her grandmother." Hilda stared at Maggie as though she'd suggested otherwise. "I know that much. I don't need any blood tests."

"Neither does Star. She claimed you. Tag, you're it."

"That's right. She came here looking for me. All the way from California, never laid eyes on each other before. Shouldn't need any more proof than that."

"Shouldn't," Maggie echoed. The story about her neighbor had a happy ending. In her line of work she'd run into plenty that didn't. "Do you think she understands that her mother's gone for good?"

"She doesn't talk about it. You mention anything about it, she acts like she doesn't hear." Hilda sank into one of the two upholstered armchairs that were fixtures in the Dugout, along with an ottoman and a couple of oak stools. Padded folding chairs were added to the mix as needed, as they were for book club. "My boys were a little older when their dad died, and they were the same way. Especially Sam."

Maggie took the other armchair. "Jimmy says she asked him what he thought it was like to be buried underground."

"Oh, dear." Hilda drew a deep breath. "What else?"

"Well, he told her he didn't think it was like anything because you weren't in your body anymore. She wanted to know if her mother was a ghost. He told her there was no such thing as ghosts. He came to me with the story because he wanted to make sure nothing had changed since the last time I told him there were no ghosts."

"Did she say anything else?" Hilda asked warily. "She's gotten right into the swing of things here, but when it comes to talking about what she left behind…"

"She told Jimmy her mother didn't mind the dark, but she hated the cold." Maggie remembered watching stoic little Star putting a clutch of colorful flowers on her mother's stark brown coffin. "He said she didn't cry or anything."

"Why would she talk to him about it and not to me?"

"Jimmy's a kid. They think alike." Maggie reached for Hilda's hand. It was like gathering a handful of sticks and marble wrapped in wrinkled doeskin. But it was warm doeskin. "She's come a long way, Grandma. In a very short time."

"It would have helped them to cry." Hilda returned the hand squeeze with a firmer grip than her arthritis should have allowed. "Seems like. You know, looking back, I…" She banished regret with a shake of her gray head. "I just don't want her to hold it all in."

"She isn't." Maggie leaned closer and sandwiched Hilda's hand between hers. "You don't need me to tell you this, but—you know me—I'm going to say it anyway. Star isn't a do-over. Your boys are men now. Their father died young, and they survived, thanks in no small part to you."

"That was a long time ago. And I don't even remember half of it. Couldn't believe he'd really left us." The older woman smiled wistfully. "I was kind of a mess there for a while."

"Well, you're not now. Your friendship has been huge for me, Hilda. Huge. I picked Bear Root totally at random. Well, pretty much. I had a few criteria, like difference and distance. But I forgot how those things can work against you. You closed the distance and showed me I'm only as different as I want to be."

"Which is less all the time." Hilda laughed. She drew her hand from Maggie's grasp and wagged a crooked finger as she stood. "You're comin' around, city girl."

"Star's going to be just fine."

Hilda turned to the window. "Look at that dog. He's got two kids, and he's in hog heaven. Uh-oh. Too high. He's gonna miss that one."

Maggie joined Hilda just as the Frisbee sailed back into view. Lucky made the catch as the pitcher strolled into the picture. In blue jeans, broad-shouldered denim jacket tapered like an arrowhead aimed at the quintessential cowboy ass, Sam made an impressive picture walking away.

He clapped a hand on Jimmy's shoulder. "Aren't you guys invited to the party?"

"What party?"

"The reading party. Did you do your reading?"

"It's not a party." Star picked up the Frisbee Lucky had dropped at her feet. "And they read books for grown-ups."

"Bor-ring," Sam sang out.

"No *duh*," Jimmy said. "Kids wanna read good books, like with fast action and super powers, maybe some funny stuff. And cool pictures."

"Nothing wrong with funny books with pictures." Star's Frisbee toss made Sam smile. "Good arm." He pumped his fist. "And Lucky *makes* the catch!"

"Lucky the Wonder Dog," Star enthused.

"No *duh*." Sam threw Jimmy's arm a loose-fisted play punch. "What do you say we give the horses a workout and then go for some ice cream?" He glanced at Star. "Three amigos."

"You got three horses now?" Jimmy asked.

"Amigos are friends," Star said. "Three friends. It's weird, nobody here speaks Spanish. Do you?" she asked Sam.

"Not much. I could have said Three Musketeers. Three riders standing around burnin' daylight." Lucky shot straight up, yipped and then lost altitude. "Yeah, you, too, buddy. Unless Ma wants you to stay and entertain." Sam flung the Frisbee and raised his voice to the window. "What do you say, Ma? Grandma?"

"Sure," Maggie called out. "I could go for ice cream and horses."

"If Jim's okay ridin' double with his ma."

"What about her meeting? What about your meeting, Ma? You read that whole book and everything."

Maggie laughed. Jimmy had never called her *Ma*. "Nobody else is here yet. We'll just put the Gone Ridin' sign on the door. That's if Sam's okay riding double with *his* ma."

"*I'm* riding double with Sam," Star insisted.

"Only got two saddle horses, ladies. Can we go, or not?"

"Come get your jacket, Jimmy," Maggie said.

"We'll take that as a *yes*. You got some long pants, little girl?"

Star looked down, as though she didn't remember she was wearing a cute pair of pink crop pants.

"She has jeans and a new pair of boots," Hilda called out. Sam jabbed a thumb in the direction of the outside stairs, and Star took off running.

"When do I get to go riding?" Maggie asked. Shielded by the window, she was feeling nervy.

"Call me any time, big girl." He thumbed his brown Stetson back from his face and grinned up at the window. "When do you want the kids back?"

"He'll be free then," Hilda whispered, and Maggie

elbowed her in the arm. Hilda raised her voice. "The discussion's over at eight-thirty."

"And that's when the conversation gets interesting," Maggie put in.

"We're not gonna walk in just in time to help clean up their party mess," Sam told Jimmy. "How does nine o'clock strike you?" The boy lifted one shoulder. "Tomorrow morning."

Jimmy grinned and nodded.

Beyond the window wooden stair treads rattled under booted little feet.

"Sam."

He stopped, lifted his eyes toward the window, the sound of his name, the way Maggie said it this time surprising them both. His gaze matched the intimacy in her tone.

"Thanks."

He smiled and gave a cowboy salute, forefinger to hat brim.

"Yes, indeed, Hilda." Maggie couldn't take her eyes off the trio until they were out of sight. "Star's going to be just fine."

Star was buckled into the booster seat Sam kept in the trunk of his patrol car for kid emergencies. Jim had been yakking up a storm since they'd turned the horses out after their ride, but the little girl had gone quiet. Tired, maybe. She'd hardly touched her ice cream. Jim wanted to know what Sam was going to do with Oreo's foal when he got bigger and whether Sam had ever coached Little League and why Sam had that leather string around his neck and could the sheriff's car go faster than regular cars. All the way back from Phoebe Shooter's place, where Sam kept his horses, the boy had kept things lively.

And Sam had kept up on his end. *Watch the stud colt grow, never coached, medicine bundle his dad had made for him, and faster than most and we're only using it now because there's no backseat in my pickup, so don't go braggin' around.*

Star seemed content enough, but quiet. She was all wrapped up in scratching Lucky's belly, the same way she'd lost herself in rubbing the white gelding he called Jaws in the downy spot Sam showed her at the base of the horse's ears. She'd kept it up as long as the horse kept his head down. For all the girl and the horse seemed to care, Sam and Jim could've been two wooden posts.

Later, when they'd gotten down from the horses on a bluff overlooking Phoebe's barn, Sam saw Star pick up a smooth, white pebble and rub it as though it might come alive or grant a wish. She tucked it into the pocket of her jeans and came to stand beside him, waiting to be lifted into Oreo's saddle before he mounted up behind her. The foal scampered alongside, cute as a kitten, but Star hardly noticed. She grabbed the saddle horn with one hand and a handful of the mare's long, silky mane with the other, rubbing it with her thumb.

"It's pretty, isn't it?" Sam remarked, reaching around her to take the reins in his left hand. "More like corn silk than horse's mane."

"It's warm."

"From the sun. Slow down, Jim." The boy was flapping his legs for more speed, bobbling in the saddle at the trot, getting ahead and getting precariously close to clunking his head on rocky ground. "Ho, Jaws." The horse was happy to oblige. "Nice, easy walk. This is where we admire the scenery. Up here, feels like we can almost reach up and touch that lucky ol' sun."

"That's a song, isn't it?" Star said quietly. "Mommy had a CD with that song on it. She said it was from a play she was in once. That lucky sun gets to roll around heaven all day."

"Sure does." He remembered the music and Merilee's pretty alto voice. He hardly ever remembered words to any songs, but now that Star mentioned it...

"The sun's so bright here. And the sky's really blue. Heaven feels like this, doesn't it?"

"That's what they claim." And he was a true believer. He'd checked out other earthly paradises—oceans and islands, desert oasis and low-country forest. Unless heaven was made of rocky peaks, cold rushing streams and pure, pine-scented air, he'd stay right were he was, thank you very much.

"Is it true? It never gets cold there, does it?"

"More like you never *feel* cold there." He thought about the way the mare's hide warmed his thighs, one of the nice things about sitting a horse behind the saddle. "Or hot or hungry or hostile, nothing like that. So it's all good. That's what they claim, anyway."

Driving the girl back to his mother's cozy nest above the store, he wondered whether he'd helped her at all. She'd gone quiet again after the talk about heaven, and he thought she might be playing it all out in her head— Merilee sailing across the wild blue yonder, soaking up sunshine, not a care in the world.

Except, maybe, for her daughter, who was very much in the world and caring—unless Sam was reading her wrong—to beat hell. And she was too young, too small, too innocent to bear such a load.

Sam was just going to have to start beating hell for her.

"Should we go for a ride again tomorrow after school?"

"Yeah!" Jim enthused, and "Yes," Star said, soft but sure.

"I've got a couple of jailbirds due to hit the road, and I gotta make one court appearance, but I should be done with all that about the time school gets out."

"Do you put the birds in jail?" Star asked.

"Not real birds, honey. It's just an expression."

"Oh, I know that. I was kidding. You call them birds because jail is like a cage."

It sounded cruel. "Sometimes when people do bad things you have to put them in a place where they can't hurt anybody."

"Then why do you let them hit the road?"

"He can't keep them in jail forever," Jim said.

"Why not? Then they couldn't hurt people."

"If they try it again, Sam can just shoot 'em."

"You're watchin' too much TV again, Jim. I don't go around shooting people."

"But you have a gun."

"Yeah, but it's mostly for show. Not for showing *off,* but for showing that you'll do what you have to do to keep the good people of Bear Root County from getting hurt. People see the gun, or this car, or even just the badge, they generally settle right down."

"But you *could* shoot if you had to," Star clarified. "Like if it was a really bad guy."

"I could if I had to, yeah."

"Or you can put a bad person in jail for a long time? Like if they try to take all your money or they give you stuff that makes you sick and they tell you the police will take you away, too, if you tell on him—you could put a person like that in jail, couldn't you?"

"I sure could." *Go easy, Beaudry.* "Do you know somebody like that?"

"Not anymore. I used to."

"What was his name? Or hers, this person?" He glanced in the rearview mirror.

She was rubbing around Lucky's stump. "I'm not supposed to say. And, anyway, it doesn't matter now. Nobody knows where we are." Sounding just as satisfied now as the dog looked, she looked directly into the mirror and smiled. "But I'm glad you're a sheriff, and I'm really glad you have a gun."

He drove to Maggie's after he dropped Star off. It was after ten, so he walked the boy to the door and stood ready to take any blame she felt like dishing out. The door opened as soon as they stepped up to the porch, and there was Maggie, looking for her boy.

"I've already heard it once," Sam said. "School tomorrow, kid's gotta have a bath, shouldn't't've kept them out this late." He nudged the boy, who darted across the threshold and past his door-tending mom. "We had a good time, but we smell like horse."

"It's all right." She invited him in with a gesture, wrinkled her pretty nose as he passed and then laughed. "Hoo-ee, Jimmy, use the industrial strength soap and lather up good." On second thought, she called after him as he scampered up the stairs. "Without getting any more water on the floor than you have to." She turned back to Sam. "The shower's leaking."

"I'm sorry."

"It probably just needs some caulk."

"Sorry about stinkin' up the place this late."

"You're kidding." She shook her head, laughed some more, laid her hand on his sleeve. "I don't smell anything but the great outdoors."

"Caulk?" He cleared his throat. She'd changed from the slacks she'd been wearing earlier into something that might have been for sleeping—black pants that could have been painted over her shapely legs and a loose-fitting animal print top with a neckline that plunged between her breasts. "What's leaking?"

"I don't know. Lila can't figure it out, either. It's not a lot, so it must be a small crack in something. I don't know whether to call a plumber or a carpenter."

"How about a Sam-of-all-trades?" He took half a step back, the better to appreciate the pale valley between those two soft swells. "I could take a look at it for you."

"Like you need another mystery to solve. It's Lila's house, so if it ends up being structural, I'll leave it up to her. But if it's just a leaky something, I should take care of it. Do you think I should try a plumber first?"

"Sure. Somebody with plumbing credentials."

"I mean, if it's a pipe or a fitting or…what?" She tipped her head, assessing. "Are you looking for an excuse to climb into my shower, Sam Beaudry?"

"Hell, no." Stupid questions deserved stupid answers. "If you're lookin' for a small crack in something, you wanna advertise for a midget plumber. Or you could go by waist size. Twenty-nine, thirty." He turned his mouth down, gave a tight head shake. "I wouldn't want to see anything bigger than thirty-two."

"Unless he's over six feet."

"Naw, they go by the pound." It was almost as hard to keep his face straight as it was keeping his eyes on hers, considering the rest of the view. Not that her face wasn't pleasing, but he was a man, after all. "The right handyman'll do you better than some big-ass plumber, but it's your call."

"I don't want to impose."

"Why not?" He'd held off as long as he could, had to look down real quick. *Mmm.* "I don't make idle offers, and I don't attach strings to my favors."

"And I don't impose."

"Well, now, we gotta be true to our don'ts." And now he had to smile. "Let me know if you change your mind."

"Thank you for taking Jimmy to—"

He laid a forefinger over her lips. "We're good, him and me." Alerted by a creaking floorboard on the porch, he glanced askance. "Hey, Lila."

"Hey, Sam." Maggie's roommate dashed between them as they stepped back from each other, a reluctant parting of the ways. "Don't mind me. I'm totally focused on the path to my pillow. Carry on, kids."

"I brought you one of Hilda's killer brownies," Maggie called after her.

"Oh, no." The tall, dark-haired woman glanced at Sam and laughed. "Thanks, Maggie, but I've learned my lesson about Hilda's killer brownies. This one's for you."

"I'm out of the shower now," Jim announced from above.

"I'll be there in a—"

FREE BOOKS OFFER

To get you started, we'll send you
2 FREE books and a FREE gift

There's no catch, everything is **FREE**

Accepting your 2 **FREE** books and **FREE** mystery gift
places you under no obligation to buy anything.

Be part of the Mills & Boon® Book Club™ and receive your favourite
Series books up to 2 months before they are in the shops and delivered
straight to your door. Plus, enjoy a wide range of **EXCLUSIVE** benefits!

- Best new women's fiction – delivered right to
  your door with FREE P&P

- Avoid disappointment – get your books up to
  2 months before they are in the shops

- No contract – no obligation to buy

2 **FREE** books
and a
FREE gift

We hope that after receiving your free books you'll
want to remain a member. But the choice is yours.
So why not give us a go? You'll be glad you did!

Visit **millsandboon.co.uk** to stay up to date
with offers and to sign-up for our newsletter

Mrs/Miss/Ms/Mr	Initials	S0EIA

BLOCK CAPITALS PLEASE

Surname

Address

Postcode

Email

Ⓜ MILLS & BOON®
Book Club

FREE BOOK OFFER
FREEPOST NAT 10298
RICHMOND
TW9 1BR

NO STAMP
NECESSARY
IF POSTED IN
THE U.K. OR N.I.

Maggie's eyes widened, and Sam followed her gaze as the naked boy approached the top of the stairs. "I can't find any pajamas."

"Jimmy, for *heaven's* sake."

"Well, I cleaned up the floor, but that was the last towel." He covered himself with his hands when he saw the full extent of his audience. "Oops."

"My fault. When I said 'see you, Jim,' he wasn't thinkin' this soon." Sam chuckled. "And I wasn't thinkin' this much. There's women down here, man."

"My mom doesn't count."

"Yes, she does." He winked at her—a rare move, but what the hell—and stepped back onto the porch without taking his eyes off her. "She does. See you, Maggie."

"See you, Sam."

She had eyes for him, too.

Maggie wasn't ready to go to bed. She stood in the dark, quiet living room feeling restless and vaguely disappointed. Why hadn't she offered Sam a drink, a cup of coffee, a late movie, some excuse to stay a little longer? Craving his company, she peered through the front window and watched the street, the occasional approach of headlights, the turnover to taillights. She felt like a lovesick, hopelessly backward teenager.

"Is Jimmy asleep?"

Maggie turned to find Lila backlit from the hallway, arms folded over the Bugs Bunny printed on her nightshirt. "Out like a light as soon as his head hit the pillow. Sam took him riding."

"Now it's your turn." Lila sat down in the closest chair, arms still folded like a woman confronting the husband she'd been waiting up for. "Jimmy's asleep, and I'm here. You go pick up where you left off, Maggie. Your conversation was just getting started."

"We were just saying good-night."

"Reluctantly. It's early yet. Call him. Better yet, go bearing gifts. There's a bottle of Riesling in the cooler that would be very nice with those brownies you mentioned."

"What was that about? *This one's for you.*"

"Hilda's killer brownies." Lila laughed and tightened her hold on herself. "You think this one's appetizing, wait 'til you meet his brother. If he ever turns up again."

"Zach? You and Zach?"

"Zach and just about every girl in Bear Root County. Zach's a heartbreaker." She leaned forward, a familiar shadow shifting in well-known territory. "But Sam's not like that. Hometown hero, Sam is. Best player on the team, best friend, always the best man, but never a groom. Do men say that? Probably not, huh?"

"No strings attached, he says, but I see heartstrings attached to a dead woman. I don't need that. I don't need a man, period. If I were lookin' for love, I wouldn't be living in Bear Root, Montana."

"Why not?" Lila reached for the switch at the base of an old slag glass table lamp.

"Why not?" Maggie studied her friend's face in the light. Was she kidding? "You tell me. With a population of one thousand, three hundred and forty-seven—"

"That's just the *town* of Bear Root. The *county* is—"

"—what are the odds?" Maggie insisted. They were big on counties in Big Sky country. "Seriously, this would be the wrong place to go looking for love. The kind they sing about."

Lila hiked one eyebrow. "I thought you didn't like country music."

"I don't. It glorifies lyin', cheatin', two-timin'—"

"Then stop singing along!" Lila laughed. "All you have to do is turn the station."

"That's what I'm saying. We only get three stations here. Where's the love?"

"So go back where you came from." With a single shoulder Maggie was all too easily shrugged off. "That's what Sam did. He saw the world, and he came back home. We're just, you know…what you see is what you get."

"What about Zach?"

"I saw what I was getting into. I wanted to be the one to settle him down." Lips in a pout, Lila shook her head. "But that's a job for Supergirl."

"Which I am not."

"You don't have to be. We're talking about Sam." Lila stood, slipped an arm around Maggie and began walking her toward the kitchen. "Take him dessert. Pick up where you left off when you were so rudely interrupted."

"He offered to fix the shower."

Lila tipped her head back with a sassy chuckle. "Oh, Maggie, that was not what he was offering when I walked in."

"I'll take the wine." Maggie put her arm around the taller woman's waist. "You never want to take a man his own mother's brownies."

At the top of a creaky wooden stairway on the back of the old courthouse building was the private entrance to Sam's apartment. It was dark back there. Anywhere else

Maggie had lived, she would have been taking her life in her hands this late at night. Here in Bear Root, Montana, climbing the back steps to Sam Beaudry's apartment—uninvited, unexpected, but not entirely unwanted—the only thing she was taking in her hands was wine and cheese. And maybe her dignity if she was wrong about the *not unwanted* part. After all, Sam wasn't like that.

The light over the back door came on before she reached the top step. The door squealed on its hinges, and he was waiting behind the screen when she got there. He was all slim jeans, bare chest and tousled hair.

Oh, God. Maybe someone had beaten her to him.

Say something intelligent.

"I was just passing by. Thought maybe you'd like to go for a walk."

You call that *intelligent?*

His face was in the shadows, but she saw his mouth slide into a smile.

"If we're gonna be passin' the bottle, let's stay away from the streetlights." He pushed the door open and stepped aside. His black hair was shiny wet, and he smelled like peppermint soap. "Come on in."

"Lila said…" She handed him the wine as she registered impressions of the man's kitchen—brown, white, Pine-Sol-scented, uncluttered, unloved. "Well, she thanks you for the offer to take a look at the shower."

"Then we'll save this until after I've fixed it." He set the bottle on a small butcher-block island without even glancing at the label.

"No, she just sent that because, I don't know…she made that remark about your brother."

"Zach?"

"The killer brownie." She gave a perfunctory smile. "Little double meaning there, I guess. All I know is, everything your mother makes is wonderful."

"On second thought, I think we'll open the wine." He opened the island drawer. "Did Lila tell you I've worked on her house before?"

"She didn't." She took a small paper bag from her jacket pocket. "I brought cheese. Couldn't find any crackers."

"I vented the new clothes dryer, rebuilt most of the porch and put in new windows on the north side." He found a basic corkscrew, closed the drawer, opened the door underneath and produced a sleeve of saltines.

"In your spare time?"

"I did odd jobs for a while when I moved back here. Like I said, Sam-of-all-trades."

"So you were serious." She liked the way he worked the corkscrew. Great hands. Strong, sure, skilled. Hand confidence looked especially good on a man.

"I'm always serious. You wanna drink with a comedian, you go over to the Man or Mare. That's where the jokers hang out."

"I made that mistake once. Ladies' night?" She glanced up from the rising cork. "Where were the ladies?"

"You didn't go in there alone, did you?" He tossed the screwed cork across the butcher block. "Aw, man. Babe—"

"In the woods!" She laughed. "Somebody shouted it out when I walked in. I didn't stay long, and it would take a lot more than free drinks to get me to go back. Talk about false advertising, the Man or Mare Saloon is no place for ladies on *any* night."

"Allgood's Emporium and the Man or Mare Saloon are the oldest commercial establishments in town." He took two juice glasses from a nearby cupboard. "Back in the day, the only women who frequented bars were whores and Calamity Janes. Have you ever seen a picture of Calamity Jane?"

Maggie bellied up to the butcher-block kitchen island across from Sam and poured the wine. "I loved the *Deadwood* series on TV."

"I don't watch much TV. Anyway, that's where the name came from."

"Man or Mare?" She slid his glass across the wooden divide.

"'Lookit that feller, just came in,'" he drawled, nodding toward the door. "'Cain't tell whether it's man or mare.'"

Maggie groaned. "That's awful."

"Here's to ladies' night at the old courthouse." He touched his glass to hers in a toast. "Next time the house'll spring for the bottle." He sipped, grimaced, set his glass down. "As long as we don't advertise and draw a crowd, Maggie gets the bottle all to herself. How long are you thinkin' of staying in Bear Root?"

She drank deeply, eyeing him steadily, imagining the feel of his glossy black hair between her fingers. "I'm not thinking of leaving."

"You've been here, what? Goin' on two years? Two years is about the average."

"Is that my probation? If I make it two years, maybe I'm out of the woods, neither babe nor dude?"

"You'll still be a babe." He watched her finish her wine. It felt like a challenge, especially when he raised his brow appreciatively as she drained the glass. He gave her a refill. "And I got nothin' against a good-lookin' dude."

"If I'm a dude, you're a boomerang. Home again, home again, jiggety jig," she teased. "What's the boomerang's average for staying away, and is he on probation when he comes back? How're you gonna keep 'em up in the mountains after they've seen L.A.?"

He studied the wine in his glass. "When an Indian goes home, they call it goin' back to the blanket."

"Who does?"

He lifted one powerful shoulder. "Just a saying. I went looking for work. I came back to get a life." His turn to give her the knowing look. "For you it might be the other way around."

"Or not. Are you doing a background check on me?"

"Not hardly." His smile always started in his eyes. "If I did, I might have to give you tit for tat."

"Now *that* might have to be the other way around."

He slapped his bare chest. "Hell, I'm way ahead of you."

They laughed together beautifully. She said, "It's not gonna happen unless you tell me what *tat* is."

"Huh-uh. It'll take something a lot stronger than this cat piss to get me—"

"Cat piss! *This* is good stuff."

"So is *tat*." He poured for her again—warm laughter and cool wine. "I'll show, but I ain't gonna tell. I don't drink much anymore, which should tell you something."

"Like my roommate, I've learned a few lessons the hard way. You don't drink, I don't assume you have a problem with it." Feeling giddy, she held her refill up to the light and peered through it. "I'm on my second glass and eyeing yours. Maybe I have a problem."

"And maybe that's what I'm checkin' out."

"You're thinking, another glass or two and maybe she'll give me the tit for nothing?"

"Now, that's cold, Maggie. We're gonna be swimmin' in maybes pretty soon. Slippery, spongy maybes." Hands braced on the butcher block, he leaned closer. "You call tat nothing?"

"I call it a pig in a poke."

"Cold and sharp." He hooked his arm behind her neck and used it like a shepherd's crook to draw her to him. "My kind of woman."

Straightening from her waist she rose to meet him partway across the island. His kiss was soft and hot, a gift that tasted faintly of fruit and fire. Clever words flew from her brain, and her fingers left the glass of wine, found his face and traced its sturdy edges with her fingertips. He tipped his head, drew a breath and helped himself again, turned the taste of her mouth into a pleasured sound that rolled around in his throat.

He touched his forehead to hers. "You're not thinking of leaving."

"I thought…"

"Yeah, me too. Thought about being with you in a private place at a quiet time. I'm glad you came here tonight, Maggie." Without releasing her he moved to her side of the island as he spoke, took her in his arms, gave her the heady benefit of his warm, bare skin. "Let me show you—" he nuzzled, breathed and whispered against her neck "—how glad I am."

"I can't…"

His quick kiss didn't exactly cut her off, for she would have left off, had he not asked, "Can't what?"

"Can't believe...I'm no babe in the woods, Sam. I'm way too—"

He gave a deep chuckle, another quick kiss.

"This isn't Man or Mare," he said as he lifted her and sat her on the island, putting them nearly eye-to-eye, a scant inch to her advantage. "This is you and me."

One of her espadrilles slipped off her heel, and she let it drop to the floor. She put her arms around his neck loosely, feeling loose and flirty, taking her turn at dropping a kiss on him. He took another, initiated it but let her make the case for loose and flirty. Unimpressed, he pressed, gradually deepening his kiss, drawing her into the pleasure of pairing lips with lips, tongue with tongue. He kissed her until she was dizzy with it, and she embraced his slim hips with her thighs to steady herself. Or hold him, or urge him on, as though she were mounted and he was on the move.

One move led to another. Her pressure, his progress. He kissed her neck and the hollow at the base of her neck, and he touched his tongue there, a small saucer that might hold some drink. She stroked his hair and his nape and his shoulders, learning him as surely as she lured him. The closer his kisses came to her breast, the harder she pressed and the softer she breathed, as though deep breaths might somehow interrupt or scare him away. He found the buttons on the back of her top and the hook on the back of her bra, and she closed her eyes to the foolishness of letting this go where he would take it, which was exactly where she would have him take it.

He kissed her shoulder as he slid her top and her strap

over its curve, and then he caught her face in his hands and kissed her until she sighed into his mouth and dropped her head back, becoming live prey offering her neck. *Take me. Consume me. I'll be good until I'm gone.*

But he didn't strike. He stroked. Gentle fingers traced her—chin, neck, collarbone, shoulders—with a feather-light touch. She opened her eyes and found him wrapped up in the movement of his hands, as though he were sculpting her. Shadow softened his face, and his body sheltered her from the light over the kitchen sink. He glanced up and caught her gaze, gave a bemused smile. She started to speak, but he shook his head, touched his finger to his lips, and took words from her mind with his steady, mesmerizing gaze. Without moving her head she followed the course of his finger from his lips to his nearly full glass of wine. He dipped his finger and took it to her lips, losing a drop midway. She felt it on her breast, and her lip quivered. He saw it on her breast, and his eyes twinkled as he painted her unsteady lips with white wine.

And he drank from her. Then he painted again and drank more while he touched the lost drop, drew a circle around her nipple and sipped from her lips. She drew a ragged breath. He dipped two fingers into the wine, dripped it on her nipple only to catch the drops with the tip of his tongue while he touched the tight, wet twin with another playful finger. It was like having jumper cables attached to her body's battery posts. She was suddenly juiced.

She squeezed his trunk with her thighs as though she would shinny up or down, use his length to transport herself to new heights or depths. But she held steady, enjoying the wonder of his easy touch. Easy until wonder turned in on her and drove itself up a notch to want more, need more, and nothing was easy.

He was sweet trouble. She was hungry for trouble. She told him so with deep-throated response to his every move. Her fingers followed the contour of his back, dipped into his jeans and dug into hard muscled flesh. He groaned and returned the favor directly, slipping his hand down the front of her knit pants, easing one teasing finger inside her. Her instinctive protest turned approving—*not that, not that, oh, yes that*—as the wrong part made the right moves, orchestrating her quick, quivering, exquisite first coming. Even as she lost herself she found the mechanics of his jeans and freed the right part, the expand-to-fill-and-then-some part, took it in her hand and gave him his turn to get lost. He was tempted. He was close.

"Help me slow down, Maggie."

"No," she whispered hotly.

"You think we can use that cracker sack for a condom?"

"Oh." She withdrew her hand, put her arms around his neck and her legs around his waist. "Do you have any?" she whispered close to his ear.

"Somewhere."

"Let's go somewhere, then."

He swept her off the kitchen island and carried her to his bed, where they undressed each other and played over and around each other until they blended into each other and danced with each other in slow rhythms and frenzied rhythms and made rhyme after rhyme after rhyme.

Chapter Seven

"I'm looking for Sheriff Beaudry."

Sam knew the voice. It went with a face he hadn't expected to see again. It had been pretty bloody the last time, what should have been the final time—bloodied by Sam. He'd do it again in a heartbeat, which was why he had to take a deep breath before he stepped into receiving, which was a fancy designation for the small area attached to his office where calls, complaints and troublemakers were taken. Phoebe was manning the desk while their part-time dispatcher, the oft-time tardy Della Marquette, took her time getting in.

"And what is your na—"

"Hello, Vic."

"Sam!" The visitor made his move toward Sam with outstretched hand, palm down, a vaguely unappealing gesture that Sam chose to ignore. His own hands felt heavy, tight, itchy—probably all in his head—and the hairy arm coming at him had about half a second to retreat. When it did, Sam lifted his gaze to the face. He watched the overeager smile dissolve. Vic squared up, set hands on hips, gave a backing-off shrug. "How the hell are you, man? I see you survived the marines."

Sam glanced at the woman in the office chair. "Phoebe, get hold of Della and tell her she's got five minutes, and then you go ahead and take that call."

"Before she gets here?" *You want me to leave you alone with this guy?*

"Now. The one time we don't take Minnie's call seriously, that'll be the time it's something serious."

It wasn't unusual for Sam to be on his own at the office. Phoebe was also part-time. If something came up, Sam would lock the door and take calls in the car. But Phoebe had a nose for trouble, and Vic stank up the place. Maybe Sam did, too, right about then. He felt like trouble. The sight, sound and smell of Vic Randone, even after all these years, put Sam in the mood to pick up where they'd left off, with Sam's knuckles throbbing and Vic's foul mouth spewing blood along with the usual obscenities.

Sam raked the man's face with a quick look. Unlike the arms, the head was losing hair. The skin looked older, but the ice-blue eyes hadn't changed. Still disarming. Until you got to know them, and then they became irritating.

"Come on back."

The invitation instantly put Vic at ease. "Thank you, Miss…*Deputy* Shooter. We're old friends, Sam and me. But it's been a while, hasn't it, Sam?"

"Keep me posted," Sam told Phoebe.

"Same here. Old friends doesn't seem quite…" Phoebe glanced between the two men as she rolled back and stood up. She wasn't one to leave anything on simmer without stirring a little. "It's something to do with that wom—"

Sam cut her off with a subtle gesture. "If Della isn't on her way, tell her she's fired."

Vic's jovial laugh turned Sam's stomach. "No-Slack Sam, we call him."

"It's personal," Sam told Phoebe. "But I'm cool. Okay?"

"Yessir. Keeping you posted, sir."

Phoebe grabbed her hat, checked back with one more glance, and closed the door behind her.

Vic folded his hairy arms over his chest and grinned. "You da man, huh? Tailor-made for you, bro. This is a job for Super Sam."

"You got all kinds of names for me, don't you?" Sam made a pretense of checking the call book before leading the way to his office. He wasn't about to put the desk between them, so he sat on it. No chair for the visitor, who wouldn't be staying long. "So, what about you, Vic? What's your game these days?"

"Took me a while to figure out where you were, which was after I figured out where she'd gone. It's been, what? Nine years?"

"Not quite."

"But she's here, right? Both my girls are here in…where are we? Bum Root, Montana?"

"You still don't read much, do you?" Sam drilled the man's smart-ass eyes with an ice-pick stare. "What do you want, Vic?"

"Well, I want my girls."

"Seein' as how they didn't tell you where they were going, I'm guessin' they don't want you."

"I know they're here, Sam. I'll find 'em." Vic grinned. "To see me is to want me."

"Right." Sam hated the self-possessed version of Vic's grin. Always had, even when they'd been friends. It had a way of popping up like a duck in a carnival shooting gallery. "I don't mind takin' you to Merilee since you can't hurt her anymore."

The duck went down. "What are you saying?"

A knock on the open door warned of another duck. Maggie stuck her head in. "Sam?"

Damn. Any time but now.

"Oh, I'm sorry." Her eyes met Sam's warning look with such an intimate, oblivious-to-all-else sheen that he moved quickly to put himself between intruding pop gun and unsuspecting duckling. "Should I meet you at Doherty's, or should we save lunch for…" She looked at Vic, puzzled a bit. "Have we met?"

"No, but we're about to. Vic Randone."

She stepped up for his hairy handshake, but her wide-eyed glance at Sam was a total giveaway.

"Whatever you've heard about me, there's another side. Merilee hasn't been herself lately, but she's been getting good medical care. I want to get her back to her own place, her own doctors, her own lovin' man taking care of her."

"Who would that be?" Sam said.

Vic chuckled, eyes sticking to Maggie. "You ever see anybody could hold a grudge longer than this guy, uh…I didn't catch your name."

"Maggie Whiteside. I was one of Merilee's nurses."

"I knew it. She landed in the hospital. That's why I haven't heard from her."

"You haven't heard from her because she's dead," Sam said quietly.

"Dead?" Vic glanced from Maggie to Sam and back again. *"Dead?"*

"She was really bad off when she got here," Maggie explained gently. "She was in a coma when we found her, so she couldn't tell us what was going on or when it started or anything. Her organs started to fail in quick succession, and there was nothing we could do."

"You gotta be…" Vic grabbed Maggie's arm. "You can't be…"

"You'd better sit. Sam, he's…" She guided Vic by the hairy arm Sam imagined himself breaking. "Sit down."

"Oh, my God. Oh, my poor Merilee." Vic's glance ricocheted again, his face drained of most of its color. "Was she in pain? Did she suffer?"

"Apparently they…" Maggie thought better of the plural. "She got off the bus and checked into the motel. The owner found her the next day. Two days?" She looked to Sam for confirmation. He wasn't in a giving mood. Back to poor, sad, shook-up Vic. "Anyway, the owner called the rescue squad. She never regained consciousness."

"She must have…" Vic looked up at Sam. "You must have seen her."

Sam gave a small shake of his head.

"You never even talked to her?" Vic's question earned him nothing more than Sam's cold stare. He turned to Maggie. "Nobody talked to her?"

"The people at the motel, but they had no idea how sick she was."

"You must have known," Sam said. "You said she was seeing a doctor."

"Yeah." Vic shifted in the chair. "Yeah, well, not like every day. She was...you know. Well, you know, Sam."

"No. I don't."

"She was a junkie. Worse than ever, I mean she was..." Vic gestured with an open hand. "Tell you the truth, we've been split up for a while. Few weeks, couple months maybe. Too long. I missed her. But, man, she just couldn't leave that crap alone." He shook his head. And then he remembered. "Where's Star?" Again the probing glances from face to face. "Where's my little girl?"

"She's safe," Sam said.

"Take me to her." Vic pushed off the arms of the chair and got to his feet. "She's probably scared to death. When did this happen?"

"Three weeks ago."

"Oh, maaan." Vic went from groaner to moaner. "Oooh, my little girl. Where's Star?"

"Technically she's in county custody," Sam said. "Her mother's dead, and her father isn't listed on her birth certificate."

"How do you know?" The moaning stopped. "You got her birth certificate?"

"It was in Merilee's personal effects," Sam told him. "There wasn't much, but she had that."

"Well, I'm here now. Where do I sign?"

"For what?"

Vic scowled. "My kid. My wife's personal effects."

"Your wife? Can you prove that?"

"You think I carry a marriage license around with me?"

"Merilee was carrying her daughter's birth certificate." Sam folded his arms. "You know how easy it is to research public records on the Internet these days? From the comfort of your own desk chair."

"All right, *common law* wife. You know how long we've been together."

"No, I don't."

"Hey, man, you left," Vic accused. A touch of whine flowed in his tone. "Remember? Didn't hardly give us no warning. Just up and took off."

"I asked Merilee to go with me."

"You didn't say nothin' to me. Maybe I wanted to join the marines. Did you think of that? We were a team. Hell, you left us high and dry."

"You got half of that right," Sam said.

"Yeah, like you never took a hit."

"*Asking* her was my worst mistake." Sam went cold inside and out, remembering the way he'd stood over the woman, offered her the ultimate choice, remembering the way she'd turned from him and walked away. "I shouldn't have asked. I should have dragged her out of that squat we were livin' in and taken her back where I found her."

"Where *you* found her? Hell, she was—"

"Instead, I left her with you. Stupid, stupid, *fatally* stupid."

"Yourself? Or Merilee? 'Cause I'll tell you what, that woman was a lotta trouble. She was high maintenance."

"Well, now she's no maintenance." Sam nodded toward the door. "You can go now, Randone. Get outta my town."

"No problem. But my daughter goes with me."

"We know for sure that she's Merilee's daughter. And Merilee told her daughter that Hilda Beaudry is her grandmother. That's why they came here." Sam took some satisfaction in the surprise Vic's eyes betrayed. "And that means she can't be your daughter."

"She can't be yours. You know damn well she was with me." Vic had the sense to glance away. "Well, whatever. You said you never talked to Merilee. The word of a seven-year-old is all you're goin' by?"

"Seven and a half," Sam amended. "She's been placed with her next known kin. You're not taking her anywhere."

Vic glanced at Maggie. "I wonder what the law will have to say in a case like this."

"I'm the law in Bear Root," Sam said. He knew it sounded trite, but it was all he could come up with in the face of an almost overwhelming urge to rip the man's eyes out if he laid them on Maggie one more time. "The law says you're not taking Star anywhere."

"We'll see." Vic sneered. "Get outta town by sundown only works in the movies."

"We'll see."

Maggie wrapped her arms around herself and stared at the open office door. *So that's him.* The picture in Star's scrapbook had been doctored up in her mind with weasel features, so he wasn't quite as unappealing as she'd imagined.

"You're unusually quiet," Sam said. "Considering."

"I'm processing." She turned to him. She wanted to hug him, but he didn't look like he wanted to be hugged.

She glanced at the chair just vacated by Randone, rejected taking a seat in favor of turning glance into stare. "You get a reality check, you want to take a few minutes to process."

"I know what you mean." He went to the window. "What did I know and when did I know it? That's the big gut-check question. Why did I let her down? Was it ignorance, or was I just plain spineless?"

"She made her own choice."

"She wasn't thinking."

"Apparently she was in love." She wondered what he saw beyond the window, but she had a feeling she wouldn't know even if she walked over there and stood beside him. "And you were, too. I'm afraid you still are, which means I need to—"

"Hey, I let her down." He shrugged. "Simple as that. If I hadn't walked away she might still be alive."

"It's not about ignorance or cowardice, and you know it." She took a seat on the corner of his desk. "You've got a massive hero complex going on, Sheriff. You join the military, you become a lawman, you defend, protect and serve. You could have saved her, but she was in love with another man, so you walked away. That's quite a burden."

"We're two of a kind, Maggie. You like to save people, too. That's why you're a nurse." He turned away from the window. "I'm not in love with her. I haven't been for a very long time."

"It doesn't matter now."

"Doesn't it?" He drilled her eyes for truth almost the way he had Randone's. "I'm free to love someone else. Are you?"

"I love my son. I'm not free to get into anything that

might not be good for him. Any relationship, anything that could be a losing proposition for him. You've got your baggage, I've got mine, Sam, and these days you pay extra for every piece, every pound, every…" She blew a sigh toward the outline of long-forgotten leakage in the old ceiling. "No, I'm not free."

"Fair enough." He moved a few folders, sat beside her on the desk and laid his hand over hers, which rested on her thigh. "That's what I like about you, Maggie. You don't beat around the bush."

"Has there been anyone else since Merilee?"

"Another bag, you mean?"

"Maybe you've almost gotten over her, but she comes back into your life more desperate than ever, and being Sam Beaudry…" She looked up at him, raised her brow. "Torches get reignited."

"Yeah, sometimes, if the carrier gets *reunited.*" He gave her a pointed look. "That was no reunion you were witnessing through the ICU window. That was a sad refrain. Merilee, Merilee, Merilee, Merilee, go gently down the stream."

"That's…lovely. Bittersweet." She turned her palm up to his. "You need time to sort things out."

"Aren't you gonna say you're here for me?"

"I'm here for lunch," she said. "Last night I was there for you and me, but last night was last night, and here we are today, and you're dealing with…" She gestured toward the door. "I wasn't prying. I didn't mean to, anyway, when you were saying goodbye to Merilee in ICU. You and Star."

"You were doing your job, watching over her. That night wasn't about me. But last night…"

"Last night came too soon." She squeezed his hand. Why was it so hard to hold back? All or nothing wasn't the only way to live. She knew a lot of sensible women. Why couldn't she, once and for all, be one of them? "It was too much too soon. We need to—"

"My baggage is all sorted, Maggie."

He wanted to kiss her. She could hear it in his voice. He wanted to verify his claim with a kiss, and all she had to do was turn her face up to him and she would soon taste the proof. She stared hard at their clasped hands and taunted herself with the temptation to jump the couch. The gun, the shark, *his bones.*

Jump, Maggie, jump.

"You're late."

Maggie jerked her head up, followed the direction of his gaze to the office door and Della Marquette. Big Della, standing there largely unfazed, big twinkle in her eye.

"But not quite late enough, looks like. Another minute and I'd be like, awww, sweet."

Maggie moved to pull her hand away, but Sam held tight. "Didn't you get my message?"

"That I'm fired? Yeah, I got it." Della nodded. "Nice choice, by the way. I approve. She'll be like, 'Chill, Sam. Take a pill. You know you're never gonna fire Della. You don't know nothin' 'bout computers.'" She slipped the strap off her shoulder and let her mammoth black purse slide to the floor. "Babysitter trouble. I'd fire her, but she beat me to it. She quit." She hauled up the bag as though she'd just netted a load of fish. "Don't mind me. Unlike some people, I got work to do."

Della disappeared, reappeared, winked and closed the office door.

Maggie's eyes connected askance with Sam's. They looked at each other for a long moment before he smiled. "She's right. I can't fire her. She knows too much."

Maggie laughed.

"And, by the way, I'm pretty fond of your son, too."

"He'd like to be your tail, which wouldn't be good for either of you. This is better." She squeezed his hand. This was good, this friends-holding-hands mode. "Do you think Randone will—"

"No." He shook his head, glanced away from her face, his eyes going cold. "No, he won't."

"Unless Star wants—"

"She doesn't. So far, I can't find any relatives, and I haven't found anything on Vic. Which only means nobody's ever pressed any charges against him." He turned back to her, puzzling. "Why would he want Star? Taking care of a kid, that's not him. Not even on his best day."

"Do you want children on your best days?" Where had that come from? She added quickly, "Does any man?"

"Who's *any man?* I like kids. Always have." He gave a humorless chuckle. "Always thought I'd have a wife first."

"Didn't we all? Funny thing about fairy tales."

"I won't ask, Maggie."

He wouldn't even clarify, but she knew, and she nodded.

"You can tell me if you need to, but I don't ask unless there's something wrong. You haven't done anything wrong."

"You don't know that."

"Sure, I do."

No, he didn't. So, yes, she needed to.

She tugged her hand from his—it didn't take much effort—and she leaned away. *Look at me, Sam. I've done some things.* "Jimmy's father was married."

"You didn't know." It wasn't a question.

"What if I did?" She stiffened. "Or what if I didn't know because I didn't ask. Because if there was something wrong, I didn't really want to know. You can't go around assuming. Some people don't—"

"Okay." He held up a hand. "I'll ask. Are you married?"

"No," she said seriously. Because he was making light, and there was nothing light about it. No ring, no discussion, no joke. "I've never been married."

"I knew that. Like I told Randone, the research is easy these days."

"You haven't checked." It wasn't a question.

"No, but I could if I needed to. I didn't need to. Ninety-nine times out of a hundred, I know a lie when I hear one." He gave a tight smile. "I don't claim to be perfect."

"But you're working on it. That hundredth time could be the killer."

"Or the time I shoot to kill."

Her easy laugh put the tension in her shoulders on notice. "Check it out, Sheriff. I'm telling the truth."

"I do have some checking to do, and I'd better get to it." He stood. "You've just talked yourself out of a free lunch."

She held out her hand. "I'll have a rain check, please."

"You got it." He gave her hand a low five, opened the

door and ushered her into the receiving area. "Della, I'm heading over to the motel."

"*Real*-ly," the woman sang out.

"Any rumors get back to me, Della…" He turned to Maggie. "I need to have a sit-down with the Gossets about Randone. He starts barkin' up Bear Root trees, he's only gonna find out they're all marked."

Chapter Eight

Maggie didn't go directly to the store. She tried to call first, but she couldn't get through. One try, one busy signal, a thirty-second self talk about minding her own business, and before she knew it she was batting on the bell pull at the Emporium.

"I'll be right with you," Hilda called out from somewhere beneath the hand-painted Dry Goods sign. Then she turned the volume down, and Maggie barely overheard, "I'll leave you to try these and see if any of them will work for you."

"No hurry, Hilda, it's just…" Her silver-haired friend appeared next to the crossed arrows pointing divergent ways to Wet Goods and Canned Goods. Maggie lowered her volume, too. "Me. I can wait."

"You don't have to," was the excessively cheery rejoinder. "That's what I'm here for. What can I do for you today, Maggie?"

"I came to give you a heads-up about…" She hated to kill whatever joy Hilda was experiencing. "What are you grinning about?"

"Nothing. Everything. You and my son."

"Sam and…" *Time out to check the bean department for spillage.* "You've had a conversation about us already today?"

"No, but we don't have to converse. He's my son. I can tell when something's bothering him, whether it's bad bothering or good bothering. And it's not about apron strings. Can you see Sam tied to an apron? Not hardly. What it is, it's…"

Taking her familiar instructive tone, Hilda stepped closer. "You have a son, Maggie. I'm like you, and then some, because I've known mine quite a bit longer. Men have no intuition whatsoever. That's why God gave them mothers. You know how they say, 'a son's a son 'til he takes him a wife'? Well, then the wife takes over supplying the intuition. Which, as we all know, is a real sense. When my sons find their personal gateway to happily ever after—I say *when* because God really does hear a mother's prayers, and you're my proof—*when* they finally make that blessed connection…"

Hilda took a breath.

Maggie was still back on "*Good* bothering?"

"Good bothering. That's you. You've been bothering him for quite a while, but it was an intermittent kind of a thing. Now it's more like twenty-four-seven. Like central heating."

"Central heating?"

"Yeah, you know, it keeps the temperature steady. You wait 'til Jimmy gets old enough to—" Hilda glanced toward Dry Goods and turned on her proprietor's smile. "Any luck?"

"These are okay." Vic Randone's head rose above a bank of shelving. "Take some getting used to. It's been years since I've worn boots." He stepped into the intersection carrying a boot box. "Hello again, Maggie Whiteside."

Maggie's throat went dry. She glanced down rather than up—he was wearing clunky man sandals—giving herself pause for composure. Had she said anything she shouldn't have?

He turned back to Hilda and gave another nod. "I should have introduced myself when I came in, Mrs. Beaudry. Vic Randone. I'm an old friend of Sam's."

Hilda stared at his hand as though he was reaching for her purse. "Ran—Randone?"

"He maybe mentioned me to you, but I hope it wasn't in the same tone he took with me." He looked at Maggie. "Not that I blame him so much with all that's happened here. You know, we both…Merilee was…" He shook his head, eyes suddenly vacant. "Feel like I've been hit by a truck. I've been looking for her for weeks. I was afraid…" He sighed deeply. "Damn. It's unreal."

"I'm…very sorry," Hilda said. "She must not have known how sick she was."

"She'd gotten so she didn't know what she was doing half the time. I tried to help." He turned to Maggie, his eyes glistening. "I did. I tried. She wouldn't listen."

"You said she was seeing a doctor," Maggie recalled. "Was that recently?"

"I don't know how recently. Like I said, she took off from me. She was like this wild bird, you know? All of a sudden she would just…" He threw his hands up, fingers splayed. "Star's been with you?" he asked Hilda. "How's she doing?"

"Real good. She's been going to school."

"She's smart, that girl. I'm glad you got her into school, into a regular routine. Sounds like you've been taking good care of her. I don't know what she's told you or how they got here, or why, or…" He gestured with the big boot box, as though it were an offering. "But thank you. Thank God, and thank you, Mrs. Beaudry."

"She came looking for me." Quietly but without the slightest reservation, Hilda declared, "I'm her grandmother."

Randone snorted. "I wonder when Merilee came up with that idea. Poor Star. God knows what she's thinking. I'd just like to see her."

Hilda folded her arms beneath her soft, round, slightly saggy bosom. "Frankly, she doesn't even want to talk about you."

"Why not? What does she say about me? Like I said, God knows what she's thinking with all that's happened. And Sam, if it's him doing the talking…" He glanced from Hilda to Maggie and back again. "All due respect, Sam doesn't know anything about us anymore. We haven't heard from him since he took off with the army."

"He was a marine," Hilda said.

"And he did call Merilee after he left, just to make sure she was okay." *Defense,* Maggie noted. Not her preferred role.

"She never mentioned that to me. She must've told him about the baby, then."

"She didn't." And this was why. Good defense gave nothing away.

"Well, see? That's because I'm her father."

"Child custody comes up at the hospital periodically," Maggie said. "Most of the time with infants, but sometimes it's an accident or the critical illness of a single parent with no known relative. That's when social services and the court step in, and that's what happened with Star. She has a guardian *ad lei tem* through the court—a professional, a social worker—and she's been placed with Hilda."

Randone looked shocked. "What am I supposed to do? This is my kid we're talkin' about. Her mother, my wife—I think of her as my wife—she just died. I got here too late, and it's killin' me. I don't know what was going on with Merilee, what's going on now…I'm…" He brandished the boot box. "I'm shell-shocked. I'm over here buying boots, for God's sake."

"You probably need a good lawyer," Maggie said.

"Yeah. Yeah, I'll get to that. Just let me see my little girl." He turned to Hilda, as though she were suddenly family. "Where's Merilee…buried?"

"I can show you," Maggie said.

Randone smiled sadly. "You're a good person, Maggie."

"I have to be at the hospital in half an hour. Do you have a car?"

"Maggie…"

"I'll call you. Book club tomorrow, right?" Maggie ignored Hilda's nonplussed stare, turned to Randone and nodded at the boot box. "As soon as you've finished here."

"I don't know what I'm doing. Thanks for your help, Mrs. Beaudry." He handed Hilda the box. "I'll wait on these. I won't be goin' hiking anytime soon." He slapped his hand over his heart, then turned his palm toward Hilda in surrender. "I need my girls. I'm lost without my girls."

"I'm sorry for your loss."

"Thank you."

Sam covered his bases immediately. Lila first. She assured him that the court and Child Protective Services wouldn't be letting Star go anywhere anytime soon. The questions were myriad, and most, if not all, would have to be answered to the judge's satisfaction. Sam's job was to carry out the judge's mandate. So far, so good.

The school would be his second stop—he had to make sure Cochran didn't let Randone sweet-talk his way anywhere near Star—but first he had a call to answer. A 510 up on County 7, and he knew exactly who was racing around up there. The Conroy kid had his old S10 up and running again. He was a damn good mechanic, but he drove like a maniac, and he was always challenging somebody to bump fenders with him.

The call took him past the cemetery, where a rattletrap Malibu with California plates set off alarm bells. As he rounded the curve that skirted the white post-and-lintel entrance, he spotted the car's owner tromping toward the new grave in town with his local guide.

Maggie.

At least it wasn't Star. He and Star were probably the

only people in Bear Root Randone couldn't sweet-talk, the only ones he wouldn't try it with. But Sam wouldn't put anything else past the man. If Star didn't want to go with Randone, there was no way in hell…

And even if she thought she did, it wasn't gonna happen.

Sam couldn't stop, wouldn't even if he could, and with their backs to the road they didn't see him drive by. Looked like they were deep in conversation. Maggie was getting an earful of BS and no doubt tempted to feel some pity for the slick son of a bitch. But if she'd taken a hint from the run-in the three of them had had earlier, she understood that Randone couldn't be trusted.

Of course she understood. Maggie was like Sam— she'd made some mistakes she was determined not to repeat. She'd learned to smell trouble, and the stink of a user was unmistakable. But she was walking downwind at the moment. Any change in wind direction, she'd catch his drift. And if she didn't…

Back off, Beaudry.

He'd already lowered his guard, exposed his glass jaw. He had to laugh just thinking about some of the dumbass things he'd said. *Free to love someone else.* Where in hell had that come from? Besides, free to love was one thing. Fool for love was a whole different animal. He tried to finish off the comparison with a particular animal, but nothing worked. Monkey, dog, mouse?

Nope. Man was the only animal capable of being that stupid.

Maggie understood grief. She'd seen it on countless faces, heard it in myriad voices, felt it inside and out, and she knew that no two people grieved the same way.

She'd cared for many patients who were ready to die, but those left behind were rarely ready.

Gone? How could she be gone? Yeah, he's gravely ill, badly wounded, elderly, frail, feeble…*but gone?*

Unbelievable.

Vic Randone was no different from any other human being touched by grief. What was on the outside had little to do with what was happening on the inside. Some people wailed. Some people stared. Some people chatted you up as though nothing had happened. Randone did all of the above and then some. There could be no doubt that Merilee was important to him.

"She didn't bring a lot with her, did she? She's always been a free spirit. Easy come, easy go," he mused as they picked their way among the plots. Maggie was scanning headstones, listening with one ear. "What did she have, some kind of little bag with her?" Vic was saying. "A few clothes?"

"They came on the bus. When you're traveling with a child, you try to think of everything he'll need. Your own stuff is secondary."

"You've got kids?"

"I have one."

"Girl? Boy?"

She glanced at the man thinking, *No names. Not for you.*

"I have a son."

"And he means everything to you, doesn't he? I can tell. Just the way you said *I have a son.* They take over your life, don't they?" He smiled easily. "Have you gotten to know Star at all?"

"She's a very special child."

"Oh, yeah, she's a doll. We named her Star because she dazzled us right from the start. From the moment she was born."

"That's quite a moment, isn't it?"

"Hey, for a guy, it's just…" He paused, stopped dead in his tracks, shaded his eyes from the sun and read something in hers. "It's humbling. You women are amazing. I missed out on the actual birth, but I was there right after they got home from the hospital."

"Really." A few more steps to the mound of fresh dirt. "This is it."

The flowers Star had brought soon after the burial were still there—desiccated but not without color— and Maggie wondered what had kept them from blowing away. One shriveled spider mum had separated itself somehow, but it hadn't escaped. It was hung up on the funeral home's marker at the head of the grave—or the small name plate was hanging on to the flower.

"This?" He squatted on his haunches, picked up a clod of dirt and crushed it between thumb and fingers. Then he stood with his back to her, brushing his fingers together, brushing one hand over his eye, cussing and rubbing some more.

"Are you okay?"

"It's just dirt. That's all it is. Dirt."

"There was a ceremony," she assured him. "A minister. Prayers and…" No tears. Somebody should come here and shed some, Maggie thought. "Well, prayers."

"It's all you can do, huh? I'll put something up. Her name on a stone."

"Sam took care of that. It's on order."

"Good ol' Sam." He rubbed his eye again. "She didn't get to see him or talk to him at all before she…"

"No."

"I don't know what Star's told anybody, but…" He shoved his hands in his pockets. "We had our ups and downs. I won't lie to you, things got crazy sometimes." A mountain breeze lifted a strand of Randone's sparse brown topknot. "Couldn't live with her. Couldn't live without her. Don't know what I'll do now."

"Give yourself some time."

"I'm gonna give myself to my little girl. Devote my life to her. That's what I'm gonna do."

Right. Maggie lifted her watch arm. "Oh, my gosh, look at the time." She said it before she actually read it. "I'm sorry, Mr. Randone, but I'm going to have to get to work."

"Vic. Please, it's Vic. I hope I haven't made you late." He was having trouble keeping up with her.

Must have been the sandals.

"I'll make it."

"It took me a while to figure out where they could've gone. Sam saw her first, it's true. I know how he felt about her, and I know that's why he left. She never said anything about him calling after that. I wonder if…" He touched her arm. "You don't think he knew she was coming?"

She gave him the hands-off look and kept walking. "That's something you'll have to discuss with Sam."

"Oh, yeah, I don't mean to go behind his back. I guess you two are…" They'd reached his car. She stood, waiting for him to unlock the door. He stood, shrugging and looking downright humble. "There I go again. I'm sorry. Sam and me go way back. Before Merilee. I know how he feels about me, and I don't blame him. Never have. He's a good man." He nodded for emphasis. "You got yourself a good man."

"If you wouldn't mind dropping me off at the hospital, it's on the west end of Main."

"No problem." He opened the passenger-side door, which wasn't locked. When they were both situated and he had the car running, he started in again. "You're not from around here, are you? You've got a different way about you. You talk different. I'll bet you're from somewhere out east."

"Connecticut. We've been here for a couple of years, though."

"You and young Mr. Whiteside."

"Yes. My son."

"Star's age? Or thereabouts, huh?"

She gave a slight nod. *Close enough.*

"Man, they grow up fast, don't they?" He allowed a moment to serve as the nonanswer to his nonquestion. Then down to cases. "How long do you think they can keep me from seeing her?"

"I think you should talk to the judge. The courthouse is right next to Sam's office." For what it might be worth she added, "Sam and Hilda are good people."

"I just want to see my little girl. That's all I'm asking. Is it too much?"

"I don't know. What I do know is that Star's doing well in Hilda's care. As far as Star's concerned, Hilda is her grandmother."

"Does she think Sam's her father? Did somebody tell her—"

"I don't know. Listen, I'm really sorry for your loss. You certainly have the right to visit Merilee's grave."

"I appreciate you—"

"But I won't be any kind of go-between. I know very little about the law, and I won't discuss my friends' business with anyone except those very same friends."

"Who was the minister?" He glanced at her. His sky-blue eyes were disarming. "The one in charge of Merilee's funeral. If you could point me in the direction of his church…I really need to talk with someone."

"Of course. Fred Munson is a chaplain here at the hospital. He's pastor of the Open Door church, which is right off Main Street. Go two blocks east and take a right." She pointed toward a spire poking out amid the tops of some lovely young aspens. "He's a sweetie, Pastor Fred. He'll help you get through this."

"I need all the help I can get. *Any* help at all would be nice." He lifted his hand from the steering wheel. "No, you've been a great help, Maggie. I didn't mean that the way it sounded. I'm just feelin' a little…short of friends here."

"Fred Munson's your man. I'm sure he'll be able to help. Tell him Maggie sent you."

Tell him Maggie sent you? Too cute. The kind of cute-ism sure to circle around and bite a girl in the butt.

Maggie resisted giving her usual look back, her bye-bye wave, because the man didn't seem to be such a bad guy. Which meant she was missing something.

Sometimes friendliness was next to foolishness.

Chapter Nine

"Hey, Ma?"

The screen door whapped shut, and Sam took a whack at the bell pull with his free hand. "You got two hungry, hungry hippos here." He gave Star's little hand a quick squeeze as he flipped the sign on the door to Closed, adjusted the hands on the Back At clock to give them sixty plus a few, and inhaled deeply. "Smell that? It's Hilda's Heavenly Hog."

"Hippos eat hogs?"

"Hungry, hungry hippos eat anything that comes out of Hilda's Crock-Pot, but Heavenly Hog is a particular favorite."

"Hippos eat *hogs?"*

"It's a game. You never played Hungry Hungry Hippos?" He was beginning to anticipate the warm feeling he got when that little face turned up to him with growing confidence. "Oh, it's cool. We'll have to get you one. It drives your grandma crazy. My brother and me, back when we were your age—" Creaky treads drew his attention to the stairs. "Hey, Ma. Got your message."

"Sam picked me up at school," Star added.

"Jim, too, but I dropped him off with Lila. Talked with her earlier. We got ourselves a situation."

"Come on up and help me set the table. I made lemonade." Hilda waited midstairs. "I found some of your old toys."

"Hungry Hungry Hippos?"

She laughed. "I'd forgotten about that one. I think it went on the endangered list."

The meal from the Crock-Pot shared in his mother's kitchen around the table of his childhood slipped an unexpected lull into Sam's agenda. A welcome sense of ease, an appreciation for all being well in the here and now. He'd felt it many times sitting at the same table, and he wanted more of it—for himself, for Star, for the three-legged dog stationed beneath Star's chair, for the slowly but surely aging woman who enjoyed feeding people up. It was a good moment, secure and simple.

He hated to complicate it.

"Star, I need to ask you about something," he began when his mother took his plate. "Vic Randone is—"

"I don't want to talk about him." Star curled her arm around the edge of her plate, as though she wasn't going to allow her last bit of pork chop to be taken away. "My mother said we were done with him, so we didn't tell anyone we were coming here in case he tried to find us."

"Are you afraid of him?"

"I don't like him." She lifted her gaze from her food to the face of a man—Sam saw it, felt it, welcomed it—she was learning to trust. "Sometimes when he was around I didn't like either one of them. Mrs. Carey let me stay with her until he was gone."

"Did he hurt you?"

She glanced away. "I just don't like him, okay?"

"You wouldn't ever want to live with him? I mean, say, if—"

"Don't you want me to live here?" She gripped her plate and searched for her grandmother. "I can help you with the store. I can do a lot of things. I helped my mother a lot."

"I want very much for you to live here." Along with her quick return to the table Hilda flashed Sam her watch-it-kid look.

"Star," Sam said gently, hand on her slight shoulder. "I don't want you to worry about this. Not one bit. But I don't want you to be surprised, either. Vic is here in Bear Root. He's staying at the motel. He came looking for you and your mom."

"All he did was make my mother get sick and mad and all kinda crazy. When the police came, I hid in Mrs. Carey's bedroom closet. She let me try on her high-heeled shoes."

"How often did the police come?"

Star shrugged. "They came one time and took her to the doctors because she couldn't stop crying."

"Did they take Vic?"

She shrugged again. "Mrs. Carey had to move to where her daughter lives."

"I wish I could meet Mrs. Carey." He smiled. "She must be a real nice lady."

"She is. After she left, we moved without telling him. He found us, though. He followed my mother after work. But then we tricked him and we came here."

"Just to get away from him?"

"To find my grandmother." She looked at Hilda. "He might try to take my legacy."

"Your legacy?"

"Her picture album," Hilda offered. "That's your legacy, right?"

"You can't tell him about it. That's my whole story so far."

Sam rubbed Star's shoulder. "Nobody can take that away from you, honey. With or without pictures, your story is your story."

"If he knew about it, he'd try to take it. We couldn't waste any time getting here. It was the only place we could think of." Star pulled the edge of her plate to her chest and looked down at the cold meat. "I mean, my mother could think of. Think, think, think, no time to waste. She said my grandmother had her own store, and she'd never seen it herself, but we went to the library and found it on the Internet." She looked up, eyes brightening with the memory. "Hilda Beaudry, prop. Not like a prop in a movie. It means somebody who has her own store. Right?"

"That's right, honey, I'm a prop." Hilda clenched her fists and bowed her arms, muscleman style. "And I am gonna *prop* you *up*."

Star's laugh was small but hopeful. "And not let him take my stuff?" Her arm retracted, slid away from the plate as though some kind of hold button had been released.

"That would make him a thief," Sam said. "I arrest thieves."

"Arrest him, then, 'cause he's always taking Mommy's stuff." She smiled. Really smiled. "Did you know she was in two movies?"

"I didn't."

"Two where you could really tell it was her. She was in the crowd in some others. I was in the crowd on *Made For Television.* Have you ever seen that movie?"

"I don't see too many movies," Sam confessed. "If it's out in DVD, let's rent it so you can show me."

"Okay." She pushed her plate back. "He'll go away pretty soon. He always does."

"Unless he gives me a reason to lock him up," Sam said.

"It's better if he goes away. Don't tell him where I live, okay?"

"He already knows. But you don't have to worry. The judge says you're supposed to stay with your grandma, and it's my job to make sure that what the judge says goes. But I wanted you to know that you might see him. As long as he behaves himself, we can't keep him out of the store."

"Can he go upstairs?"

"No, he can't. That's why we have that sign at the bottom of the stairs," Hilda said as she left the table again. "It tells people this is a private residence."

"Meaning this is your home, and you get to say who comes in and who stays out," Sam explained over the creaking of the door and the rattle of pan on rack.

"Can he go to my school?"

"Nobody gets into a school these days without approval," Sam said. "Does he come looking for you very often?"

"Just me? No. It's my mother. But she always got sick from him, and I don't wanna get sick like that." She lowered her voice to confide, "There's good medicine, and there's bad medicine. Did you know that?"

"I know it now," Sam said. "I can tell right now, I'm gonna learn a lot from you, Star. We're going to talk to Lila, and I want you to tell her everything you've told us about Vic."

"I don't wanna talk about him."

"I don't, either, honey, but we have to. Lila's like your legal guardian right now, and she has to be able to tell the judge why you shouldn't be with Vic."

Fear came hard and fast. "Be with?"

"He says he's your father." He hated saying the words, but he couldn't allow her to hear them from anyone else first.

"He's not my father." For good measure she turned to Hilda. "He's not my father."

"Did your mother ever tell you about your father?" Hilda asked gently.

"A lotta kids don't have fathers. At this school here they mostly have fathers somewhere, but at my old school, there were some of us who didn't."

"Even here in a small town, stuff happens, kids end up without a father," Sam said. "My dad died when I was a kid. It's not the end of the world. My brother and me, we had our ma." Who returned to the table on cue. "This fine lady right here. And now you've got her, and I've got her, and she's got me, so you've got me. That's how it works." He touched the back of the child's little hand. "Slick, huh?"

"What about your brother?"

"Well, Zach's another story. If he needs us, he knows where we are." He glanced at his mother. "Wish we could say the same."

"I heard from him a few months ago."

"Twelve months ago, Ma. Some people call that a year." He shook his head. "Don't look at me like that. There's never been a time you couldn't reach me even if you didn't know exactly where I was. And I called you a lot."

"Not so much when you were out there in California."

"You gotta let people know where you're going, and you gotta check in." He winked at Star. "Rule number one."

"I'm not going anywhere," Star put in. "I wanna stay here with my grandma."

"I don't want you going anywhere at all by yourself," Sam told her. Smart kid, getting them back on track. "I told Mr. Cochran about Vic. He's not to take you out of school no matter what. You say he's not your father, he's not your father. Now, do you smell something a whole lot sweeter than this conversation?"

"My grandma is the best cook ever."

"My Rhu Bars," Hilda said. "We'll give them a few minutes to set."

"She doesn't have to advertise to lure in the customers. All she has to do is start cookin' and open up the windows. You know what they say about Grandma's Crock-Pot chops?" Star shook her head. "They're piggin' out in Paradise on Hilda's Heavenly Hog."

"Is that where Mommy is?"

"Yes, ma'am."

"She doesn't eat meat."

"She doesn't pig out, either." Sam chuckled. "In Paradise I bet you get to have dessert even if you haven't eaten your supper."

Maggie was hungry when she got off at seven. She'd been thinking about the pizza she'd promised Jimmy, and when she saw Sam sitting on the bench outside the hospital's front entrance, she smiled big, betting on mental telepathy. He wore off-duty jeans and looked good enough to eat, but when he looked her in the eye, braced his hands on his thighs and pushed himself up, he wasn't smiling back. Since she didn't like losing, it was a good thing she was betting against herself.

"You got a few minutes?"

"For a friend? All the time in the world. Can you have supper with us?"

"I had supper early at Ma's." He stuck his thumbs in his pockets, glanced toward the nearest mountain—the one the Indians called Big Bear, non-Indians called Dreyer's Peak—and back again. "Look, I can't tell you to stay away from Randone. You wanna show him the sights of Bear Root, that's up to you."

"Thanks for not telling me what I already knew, Sheriff." She smiled. He had that Serious Sam look in his eye, and she looked for her cheekiness to inject a little sparkle.

It didn't happen, so she dropped the smile. "I don't know who reported me to the authorities, but I went over to the store to see Hilda—thought I'd give her a heads-up about Randone since you were headed for the motel—and he was there shopping for shoes. He wanted to visit Merilee's grave, so I showed him where it is. I thought it was better than—"

"There's no *good* with Randone, so forget about *better.* But that's just my opinion."

Serious Sam was one thing. Insensitive Sam was something else.

"When you're not there when somebody dies, it's almost impossible to believe it at first. You see a grave, the reality begins to set in. He was clearly shaken by it." Not that she intended to defend Randone, but a point had to be made, and Nurse Maggie was there to make it.

"Yeah." *Point not taken.* "I don't know what he's up to, but here's another reality for you—Star won't even say his name. I don't want him anywhere near her."

"If he's her father, you might have to—"

"No way." He pointed his index finger a few scant degrees north of her face. "You ask Star. Randone is not her father."

"Sam." *Lower the tip of that finger one iota and I'll have it for supper.* "You said you didn't know—"

"I didn't know she was pregnant." He slid down the course of a sigh and settled on the bench again. "He's a user, Maggie. You can take my word for it, or you can find out for yourself." He looked up, gave a thin smile. "Easy way, hard way. Take your pick."

"I'm on Star's side." She sat down next to him. "I'm on *your* side, Sam. Granted, I don't know the man, and you do. Or *did.* What do you think he could be up to? What possible use could she be?"

"He came looking for Merilee. He's had a stranglehold on her for years, and she finally got away from him. For good." He leaned forward, braced his elbows on his knees and laced his fingers together. "I hope it's good. I hope she's at peace, and I hope…" He gazed absently down Main Street. "Do you think you get to see how things go for the people you leave behind? Maybe help them out a little bit, like some kind of…"

"Guardian angel?" She remembered the children's song she was now destined—doomed—to associate with Sam's old flame. "Life is but a dream."

"Or a nightmare. From what Star told me today."

Maggie stiffened. "Did he…did he abuse her?"

"Abuse Star? She didn't say. It was all about her mother. He made her sick, she said. Made her act crazy, made her…" He shook his head. "He was pumpin' her full of drugs, Maggie."

"She was *using* drugs."

"You weren't there." He switched elbows for hands. "I should've been. When Star was born, I should've been there."

"It would have been nice if *somebody* had been there. Randone said he wasn't."

"See? He's nobody's damn *father*."

"He didn't say why he wasn't. He says he kept trying to help her. Merilee, I mean."

He glanced at her, thinking *You believe that?* Then he glanced away, and she wondered whether he thought he'd seen the answer written somewhere on her face.

He shrugged. "So he comes after her, he finds out she's dead, he sees the grave, he's done. Now he leaves."

"He wants to see Star." Maggie covered his hand—part of it, anyway—with hers. "Maybe he just wants to share the sorrow and ask her who she wants to be with. A man in his position, that's probably what he'd do. He can always say he gave her the option. He must know how she feels about him."

"We'll see."

"What about a paternity test?"

He looked at her as though she'd taken leave of her senses. "She's seven and a half years old, and her father's still unknown. Randone's been hangin' around them, and he's never stepped up to the plate. Why would he be so anxious to do it now?"

"Would you?"

Surprise turned to scowl. "I'm on deck takin' practice swings. I don't need a paternity test. Merilee told Star she was going to see her grandmother. That's enough for me."

"That's admirable, Sam. And it doesn't surprise me." For lack of reception, she withdrew her hand. "He says he has a right to see his daughter. I told him he ought to call the court, talk to the judge, maybe even a lawyer. Proper procedure. If you've got him pegged right, he's not going to do any of that. Certainly not all of it."

"Unless he thinks he can get something out of it. Little Star thinks he'll take everything she has, which sure isn't much."

"What did he get out of Merilee?"

He gave a dry chuckle. "Everything she had."

"She could've had you. You could've been the one trying to fend off her demons all this time. Coulda, woulda, shoulda?" He questioned her with a look, and she answered. "She *gave* him everything she had, Sam."

"Everything but Star." He stood up quickly. "I'm

sure Vic appreciates all your advice," he said as she followed suit. "Nice display of Western hospitality. Trouble is, that's not what we're known for."

"I can vouch for that. Dudes have to prove themselves. I was practicing being neighborly. *That's* what you're known for."

"Randone isn't a neighbor."

"You say *beware,* and I say *be fair.*" Which reminded her of a song, so she conducted herself with a wagging forefinger. "You say bewa-are. I say be fa-air. Let's call the whole thing off." She smiled apologetically. "I really have to get home. Are you sure you couldn't go for some pizza?"

Try as he might—she could see both, the try and the might—he couldn't banish the light of a squelched smile from his eyes. "Tell Jim I'll take them riding again. I've got some time Saturday." He nodded. "What about you?"

"On Saturday?"

"Any day. You name it, I'll work it out."

"I could bring you some cold pizza later tonight."

Now he smiled. "You could. I really like it that way for breakfast."

"I like to be home for breakfast."

"We can work that out, too. Can I give you a lift?"

"I'm a dedicated walker. Keeps the weight off." She laid a hand on his chest. "I'm on your side, Sam Beaudry."

Maggie loaded six pairs of boys' size-ten jeans into the washing machine. Six dirty jeans meant her boy was down to two clean pairs. She checked the whites. Only three pairs of dirty briefs. She was going to have to talk to him again about changing underwear. Did little boys know no shame?

If she'd had a brother, she would know these things. Or a husband, maybe. Her father had been distant, died young. So it was up to her son to teach her about the wiring of the male brain.

Lila joined her in the cellar laundry room and plunked a basketful of clothes on the concrete floor. "Just in case you need a few things to fill out a load. I ran into a little spaghetti sauce last time I wore—"

"I'm happy to do all the laundry in exchange for dishes. Or bathrooms," Maggie proposed. One of Lila's requirements when she'd advertised for a housemate was the divvying up of household chores, but Maggie was better with details.

"You wouldn't be happy with the way I do bathrooms," Lila said. "But I'll take your dishes for my laundry. I don't know how you do it, but stains don't have a chance against you."

Maggie laughed. "I have a nine-year-old boy."

"And you're a lucky woman." Lila leaned her back against the quiet dryer. "I talked to the judge today. She said Sam called about the unexpected appearance of Star's mother's main squeeze. He claims to be her father?"

"Star wants nothing to do with him, so that should tell you something."

"Better if *she* tells me something," Lila said, and Maggie took the hint. Lila was Star's personal advocate. Hearsay wasn't going to cut it. "Star said she didn't have a father when we did our intake. She has a grand-mother who isn't related to her mother, but she has no father. So we know Merilee wasn't getting state assistance, because they would have gone after paternity."

"We know she was a waitress, an aspiring actress, did some work as a movie extra."

"Do we know if this guy contributed anything?" Lila asked.

"Besides the high life?" Maggie shook her head. "She was carrying a paycheck with her that she'd already endorsed over to him. She must have changed her mind and decided to run."

"Have you ever run across a worse-timed death? The woman left more loose ends than a spider on crack." Lila shrugged off Maggie's admonishing look. Maggie was always defensive of the dead and dying. "I'm just saying, she could've left a note."

"You make a good point, girlfriend." Maggie squinted one eye and wagged a mock-professorial finger. "Loose as the ends might be, they have to add up to something."

"That *is* a good point, isn't it?"

"And Sam's probably right. The love of a father for his child doesn't quite fit the equation."

"No, but blood generally trumps love. Whoever proves paternity…"

Maggie scowled. "Will the court order tests?"

"Law enforcement brings the child to protective services, which is me. I go to the court with options and recommendations, and the court places the child. The child gets a guardian—in this case, that's also me—and I look after the best interest of the child while we all try to figure out what that is. The law gives natural parents first dibs. So Randone goes to the court and makes that claim, but there's no proof…" Lila spread her hands. "The court orders paternity testing. If Sam comes forward, they both get tested. Obviously, in the absence of the mother's word on the father's identity, these guys don't ask, we can't tell. In that case, we try to come up with the best placement for the child."

"Placement," Maggie echoed in disgust. "It sounds like you're talking about furniture."

"Hey." Lila lowered her chin and stared until Maggie met her gaze. "You want my job? It's like trying to play chess, and all you get to move are the pawns."

"I know. You have to be a professional, first and foremost."

"If you and Sam weren't involved as professionals first, we wouldn't be having this conversation." Lila lifted a shoulder. "Shouldn't be having it anyway. Technically. She's a minor. But he's the sheriff, and you're Nurse Maggie."

"And technically Randone isn't involved unless he petitions the court for custody, right?"

"Right. The court doesn't recognize him unless he comes forward or somebody points the finger."

"What does he want?" Maggie pondered aloud.

"That's the big Final Jeopardy question." Lila's fingernail clicked *tap tap tap* on the top of the dryer. "Oh, the pressure." She laid her tapping hand on Maggie's shoulder and gave a sympathetic squeeze. "Write your answers down before time's up. Winner gets a Star."

Come again, Maggie.

Sam didn't mean to be looking out the front window as he was gathering up folders full of forms speckled with his chicken scratch. If she showed up, he wouldn't see her out front. It wouldn't be a sheriff's office call. She'd be knocking on the kitchen door, standing on the landing in the dark. She wouldn't be looking for Sheriff Beaudry. She'd be looking for her man, Sam.

Easy way, hard way, take your pick.

He hadn't given her much to choose from, really. One man's word over another's. Nothing hard about that. Pick the one that rings true.

Him or me.

Damn. Was that it? She'd just barely met the man, and Sam was saying, *Take your pick?*

No way. Hard or easy, my way or the highway—Sam wasn't the ultimatum kind of a guy. If she came, his door was open. The light was on. If she didn't come, hey, some other time, maybe.

He didn't see her, didn't hear footfalls on the wooden steps or the turn of the knob he'd left unlocked. He felt her. She was there, present in his space, breathing his air, changing everything. He felt the difference, followed it to the kitchen and found her waiting.

He took her in his arms and kissed her, his skin sizzling beneath his shirt where her hands blazed their trail around his waist and up his back, sinking into her embrace, lifting her in his. Hard and easy both. His way and her way both. Their lips together, their kiss, their hearts thumping *yes-yes, yes-yes.*

And there was no time like the present.

His hand in her hair, her cheek against his neck, two smiles in the dark.

"Where's the pizza?" he whispered.

She gave a throaty laugh. "Search me."

He leaned back, took her face in his hands and smiled. "Make it easy on yourself. Tell me what you brought for me this time."

"It's my right to remain silent."

"Good." He kissed her mouth open, tested and tasted, teased and tongued while he slid his hands over her shoulders between her jacket and her blouse. He pushed her jacket off, turning it inside out like a banana peel, freeing her shoulders, tying her arms. "We'll see how long that lasts."

She pressed her lips together and challenged him with a sassy look. He gave it back to her, minus the sassy. He didn't do sassy.

Buttons. He loved finding buttons on a woman. He liked finding them on their clothes, too. Liked the way they eased through the holes with the flick of a thumb and forefinger. And while he was at it he liked the front clasp between her breasts. He turned the backs of his fingers to her skin and slipped them under one loose cup, brushed her nipple barely, just barely, which was all it took to make it bead up. And suddenly she was quivering on the intake of breath, his hand and her bra falling away, her breasts emerging like two needy, avid, curious creatures.

"S-Sam," she whispered.

He lifted his gaze and found huge, hungry eyes looking to him for anything but the next word from a familiar line, anything but wit or wordplay aimed at bringing anyone to heel. She was trusting and trembling. She was there.

And so was he.

He slid her jacket down her arms and let it fall to the

floor, freeing her to reach around his neck and draw close, get steady, let him know without saying what she'd brought him. Save the banter. Save the games. He lifted her, and she wrapped her legs around him so he could take her to his bed and treat her to all the tenderness he felt for her.

They undressed each other quickly, eager to touch and taste, each looking to turn the other inside out with wanting and willingness. His hands made her feel things in places he couldn't touch. Her mouth made him hungry in places she couldn't feed. But they touched and kissed and suckled and drove each other to places beyond food and drink, flesh and blood, mountains and valleys and air. He took her to the edge and let her fly like a kite tethered to his hand, up, down, up higher and down a little, up again until he could contain no more, postpone no longer, and off they went together.

"You're full of surprises." He held her close and touched the parts of her he saw every day—her fingers, wrist, neck, chin—public parts that he would never again see the same way anyone else saw them. He knew them better now. "That's what I like about you, Maggie. One of many things. They're piling up."

"You know what I like about you? Besides the obvious." Her hand stirred over his chest. "It turns out, you're easy to talk to. I thought you were never going to talk to me."

"I didn't know you wanted me to." He nuzzled her hair. "If I'd known that was all it was gonna take, I'd've talked my head off the minute you stepped off the train.

And here I've been playin' it cool and sleeping alone for two long years."

"Playing it cool for me?"

"Don't act like you didn't notice. I caught you noticing a time or two. But you're a little head shy. A guy makes a move toward you with a bridle, you throw your head up and make him back off. You like to be the one doin' most of the talking."

"I don't trust silence."

"You need to work on that. Silence is golden."

"Or dark with secrets. Or still as death." She lifted her head, rested her chin on her hand. "It started with Merilee, didn't it? We really started talking. She was the critical intersection for us."

He groaned.

"No, it's true. You had to—"

"Geez, Maggie, cut me some slack. I might be a little slow, but still as death? That's harsh."

"Not you. I just meant…" She drew a deep breath and sighed. "Merilee was the one who was full of surprises. Not me. When somebody hands you a big surprise, the decisions have all been made. And there you are, blindsided." She touched his chin. "I really can't remain silent, and I don't get off on surprises, just so you know."

"And I'm not hiding anything, just so you know. What you see is all there is. But you gotta look with more than just your eyes."

"My pleasure." Tracing the line of his jaw with her forefinger, she promised herself not to deny any of her senses the pleasure of Sam. "I didn't stop seeing Jimmy's father when I found out he was married. I was in too deep, and he said he was almost out of the woods. And those are truly opposing images, aren't they? I've tried on a hundred excuses, but none of them exonerates me."

"Did you tell him you were pregnant?"

"I did. I'll never know whether that was what sent him back to his wife, and neither will Jimmy." She laid her head back and sighed. "We haven't really talked about it. I'm a coward that way."

"You don't lie to him."

"No."

"You can't tell him what you'll never know."

"That's true." She rolled her head side to side. "I just hope he never decides to go looking for him."

"Jim's gonna be a man someday, Maggie. He'll make decisions for himself."

"I know. But it's those damned surprises." Her voice dropped. "I wish I hadn't told him. It doesn't bother me anymore that he walked away from me. Good riddance. But I still want to kill him for walking away from Jimmy."

He said nothing.

"You didn't know."

"I'll tell you what I *did* know," he said quietly. "I knew what was goin' on between Vic and Merilee before I saw it, recognized it, got her to admit it to my face. I had to be told straight out. Otherwise I couldn't leave."

"There was a lot going on."

"Too much. I joined the marines half lookin' to get my head blown off."

"Sam!"

"Yeah, I figured getting a whole new head would be easier than emptying out the old one. And it was. Nothing kicks a bad habit better than picking up a few good ones. Maybe it wasn't so much a matter of getting a new head as getting the old one back on straight."

"I like the way it fits." His neck felt warm and strong against the back of her hand. Fingertips lightly trailed from earlobe to collarbone betrayed a rare vulnerability, and he gave a laugh she hadn't heard before— boyish and goose-bumpy. She stretched to kiss what she'd tickled, settled back and delighted in her power to get a rise out of him. *Ah, yes. Let me count the ways.* "I don't know why any woman would choose—"

"It doesn't matter." He touched his lips to her hair and spoke warmth. "Your choice is the only one that means anything now."

"Besides Star's," she amended after a long, sweet, self-indulgent moment.

There were some people she didn't mind sharing him with, and she could help him in so many ways. She shifted onto her hip, turning to him, embracing the choice she'd made and he'd welcomed. Being together.

He greeted her turn with his hand, reaching to touch her. She met him, palm-to-palm, laced her fingers with his and clasped hard, two into one. "It would help if we knew what Randone's up to. That way we could anticipate what he might do rather than having to wait until he makes a move."

"I'm looking for contacts."

"You have one right here in town." She squeezed his hand. "Me."

"You?"

"He's tried to pump me for information. Two can play at that game."

"I told you, Maggie, it's no game."

"Just an expression. He says he's coming into some money. I don't know what that's about, but I might be able to find out."

"If you had wings, you might be able to fly." He drew their clasped hands to his chest. "I've asked you to stay away from him. Now I'm tellin' you, Maggie. You start playing detective, you'd better have a license. Otherwise, heads will roll."

"Mine?"

"Just an expression." He carried her hand to his lips. "But don't test me, woman. Don't test me."

Chapter Ten

Maggie accepted the role she was offered in Sam's game plan, which included chaperone rotation. Star was not to be left alone on the streets of Bear Root, and Jimmy didn't count as a chaperone. When he questioned the need for his mom to meet him after school and why they were taking the long way around, why they always walked, why they were walking so fast, why they were going to the store, and why couldn't he go riding with Sam, too, Maggie answered honestly, if not completely, while she kept a lookout for Randone's car.

She didn't expect to find the man waiting on the bench on the porch at the Emporium.

Star's little body stiffened. Maggie could feel it in the way she clutched her hand.

Vic watched them approach. His face crumpled

slowly, and tears welled in his eyes. He covered them with his hands, bowed his head momentarily, and then looked up, smiling at Star through his tears. He was either a hell of an actor, or he really was glad to see her.

But the child was unmoved. She stood rigid and silent.

"It's okay," Maggie said quietly and urged the children toward the steps.

"Hey," Randone cooed, getting slowly to his feet. "My little shining Star, I'm so glad to see you." He took a single step. Star's hand tightened around Maggie's fingers. "And I'm so sorry we lost her, honey. I should have been with her. With you. I swear, if I'd known she was sick like that…" He took another step, and Star stepped back. "I don't blame you for being mad at me, honey."

"What's going on?" Hilda demanded behind the screen door.

"I was just about to go into the store, and here comes my shining Star. I just lost it. I'm sorry." He passed his hand over his forehead as though it ached and moved aside without taking his eyes off Star as Hilda pushed the door open. "Maggie took me up to the cemetery, showed me where they buried her. I still can't believe it."

Star gave Hilda a plaintive look. "Can I go up to my room now?"

"Sure." She turned her arm into an archway and made safe passage between herself and the screen door. Star scrambled up the steps and bolted inside.

"There's all kinds of fresh fruit in the kitchen. Produce truck came today. You and Jimmy—" Hilda signaled for the boy to fall in behind Star. He sagged his shoulders, tipped his head back, rolled his eyes and plodded up the steps in reluctant compliance. "Help

yourself to that box of drumsticks in the freezer, too."
Jimmy perked up and picked up his pace. Hilda closed
the door behind him, folded her arms and stood guard.

"I take it he's yours." Vic offered Maggie his doleful
smile first, then spread the love Hilda's way. "The way
you've—*both* of you—have taken her in and made her
obviously feel welcome is just wonderful. Especially
under difficult circumstances. I don't want to upset her,
but, uh…" He shoved his hands into the front pockets
of his oversize jeans. "Well, we've got some time. They
rent rooms by the week over at the Mountain Mama
Motel. I just want to be able to see her. I know she's mad
at me, but she'll get over it."

"Why would she be mad at you?" Hilda asked.

"She probably blames me."

"For what?"

"Everything that's happened." He lifted one shoulder. "She's a kid. What does she know? I look like the
bad guy, but her mother had some serious problems.
What do you do? We both love Merilee. I'm not gonna
tell it like it is, not to a kid that age. You know what it's
like, loving an addict? It's hard. It's so damn hard."

"It's about Star now, Vic," Maggie said. "It's all
about Star."

"Absolutely." Vic bobbed his head repeatedly. "Absolutely."

"And she's uncomfortable with you right now,"
Maggie said.

"I was only with her for a minute here. Not even that.
She's heard people trash-talkin' me lately. Sam, no
doubt, and Merilee before him. That's not right." He
slapped his hand over his chest. "I *am* her father."

"Are you willing to let her decide?"

"Who her father is? Hell—"

"When she's ready to see you," Maggie said.

"Maybe she'd see me if you came along with her." He glanced from Maggie to Hilda and back again. "You can't leave something like this up to a kid. If we spend a little time together, I know she'll soon be just fine with me."

"I've got customers." Hilda turned away and reached for the door handle.

"I'm a customer," Vic said. "You take cash, don't you?"

"Absolutely." Hilda gave Maggie a furtive but pointed glance, then disappeared behind the clacking screen door.

"Are you looking for custody of Star?" Maggie leaned against the porch rail. "Total responsibility of a seven-year-old child?"

"I might be looking for a wife to go with the child. Care to apply for the position?" He chuckled. "Hey, I'm kidding. But we both have kids, and since we're not from around here, we can both think of better places to raise them. If only we had the money, huh? Must be why you came to this berg. Low cost of living? Low interest, low expectations, low everything except altitude."

"I'll tell you what, Vic, kids are high maintenance."

"Don't I know it," he claimed. And reclaimed the bench.

Maggie decided against sitting—even though he'd left exactly half the bench open—and for prying. Straight out.

"Why isn't your name on Star's birth certificate?"

His eyebrows bobbed. "Merilee liked to think she

was in control. Furthest thing from the truth, but women do hold certain cards these days when it comes to kids."

"You wanted parental rights?"

"I didn't push. She wanted to say the baby was all hers? Fine with me. But I was there for my girls." He looked her in the eye. "I'm here now."

Right. And she would get what she could out of him.

"Have you talked to the judge?"

"Not yet. I'm looking for legal counsel. I don't know anybody around here, but I've got plenty of contacts. So I'm callin' around." He stood. "You wanna get some lunch? Dinner?" He nodded toward her wrist. "What time is it?"

"I can't." But she wasn't abandoning her post. "Didn't you come to spend some cash at Allgood's Emporium."

"I came to see Star. But that's not gonna happen unless I start raisin' some hell." Hands in his pockets again he sidled closer. "Or get you to help me out. You're a caring person."

"I'm a caregiver. That's my job."

"You took care of Merilee, and now you're helping out with her daughter. People like you deserve a special place in heaven." He smiled. "And big rewards here on Earth. How well do you get paid for your job? I'm not just being nosy. I'm about to come into some money. Big money."

"How nice for you."

"And for Star. You, too, you just say the word."

And the word was reward? Money? Star? She didn't see the fit, but he was after something. A missing piece. And if Maggie thought long and hard about what he'd said, she might find a clue in it somewhere. She'd met his kind before.

* * *

Randone hadn't been gone long when Sam came to get her for the horseback ride he'd promised. She recognized the roar of his old pickup, and she was out the door of the Emporium just as his boots were hitting the gravel. She bounded down the porch steps the way Star had run up—drawn to a stalwart Beaudry. Sam stood waiting, and she couldn't look away. He was beautiful. No oversize overalls for this cowboy. His jeans skimmed his long, lean legs as though they'd been cut to fit. The Red Sox T-shirt peeking out from the denim jacket made her smile. He touched the brim of his Stetson, acknowledging her approval, which turned her smile into a laugh. How could he know?

By the look in her eyes, of course.

She almost kissed him right there on the street. Wanted to, but didn't. Instead, she touched the hand resting on the pickup door. "I've got the kids all situated, and I'm ready to rock and roll."

"I'm the lock-and-load guy. You must be lookin' for that guitar picker down the street."

"Nope. Lock-and-load guy meets rock-and-roll girl. Much more interesting match." She play-punched him in the gut. Man, he was solid. "Let's ride."

But an hour into the outing, her swagger had deserted her. Not that the company wasn't all she'd expected or the spring green meadows and pungent pines weren't breathtaking. It was the lower half of her body that wimped out on her, but she'd be damned if she was going to cry *Uncle Sam!* He was having too much fun showing off his good-guy cred by riding circles around her on his flashy white horse. She didn't want to go fast, but she wasn't going to tell him that. She wondered how likely the black-and-white mare would be to dump her the minute the tag-along colt said he was hungry—which could happen anytime, knowing boy babies—but she wasn't going to ask.

They were moseying—finally!—in the shade of a red clay cutbank when he circled to her side and asked, "How're you doing?"

"You tell me." Her smile probably looked as strained as she felt.

"You said you knew your way around a horse. I have a feeling what you meant was, you can name the parts."

"My legs are stretched around the wide part."

"But you're not complaining." His smile was almost as tender as her wide part. "That's what I like about you, Maggie. More heart than brains."

"Takes one to know one."

"Damn straight." He reached to touch the high point of her cheek and then her nose. "You need a hat," he said as he took his off and put it on her. "Fits good. That's a big head you've got there, woman."

"Something else we have in common." She offered a quick, tight smile. "They're piling up."

"I like the differences just as well. More, maybe. Good example, your ass is softer than mine."

"No kidding." She leaned back as far as she dared and gave his rear view an appreciative once-over. "People call you a hard-ass behind your back, Sheriff Beaudry. But half of them mean it in the nicest way."

His playful wink was his only comeback.

"I went riding a lot when I was a kid. Two or three

times at least. That's a lot when you're paying by the hour. Do I look terrible?"

"You look beautiful. Not terribly secure, but beautiful." He nodded toward a stand of timber. "If you can make it up another hill, there's something really special I want to show you."

"I'd better have more than one more hill in me or I won't be able to get home."

"We'll get you home." He leaned over the saddle horn and patted the white gelding's neck. "Won't we, ol' man?"

"No more trotting, okay? Oh, no, we're trotting." And she was bouncing like a bowl of Jell-O. "I hate you, Sam Beaudry!"

"No, you don't," he called back.

"Your hat!"

The white horse broke his stride. Sam circled his mount, and Maggie nearly flew over the mare's ears with the change of pace, but she was laughing. "Got'cha!"

Her big head filled his hat just fine.

At the top of the next slope she saw what he meant by *special*. Long cloud shadows dappled the swaths of pale green grass that meandered among granite outcroppings, scrub pines and splashes of mountain wildflowers in the valley below. Tall pine hugged the base of foothills, marched into their folds and trailed into the skirt of Big Bear Mountain.

"Oh, Sam. Now *this* is beautiful."

"Worth comin' home to." He coaxed his mount with the subtle shift of his body. "This is my slice of heaven," he said as the horses picked their way down the gentle slope. "Forty-seven acres of it, anyway, and you're not even lookin' at the best part yet. You can't see it from here, but there's an access road below that bluff. We'll go back that way. We took the scenic route gettin' here from Phoebe's place."

"And it gets better?"

"You'll see." He pointed toward a trio of mule deer at the edge of a stand of ponderosa pine. "Some of the neighbors."

Six legs swished through hock-high grass dotted with patches of flowering clover, nodding yellow columbine and sprigs of blue flax. It was like a quilt fluttering on the soft evening breeze.

"Better than this?"

"You'll see."

Surprise after surprise materialized as they drew closer to the tall pines. The ephemeral spring blooms of the prickly pear cactus were hidden in the grass. Two swiftly flowing streams made their way in and around the rocks and trees. Bird calls multiplied. Worldly noise faded and complications receded, out of earshot, out of sight, out of the moment.

The ride continued past the pines that curtained the loveliest of surprises—the site of Sam's future home. A small lake glittered like a jewel, pine trees on one side, meadow on the other. The only vestiges of human incursion were the bones of a barn, and it was hard to tell whether the structure was coming or going.

"This is it," Maggie said.

"It is, but there's more. I've never showed it to anyone."

"Show me," she implored, suddenly enamored of secrets and thinking, *Get thee behind me, sore bottom.*

"The thing is, you gotta use your imagination. That's why I don't show it to anybody. If they can't see it, they might try to make it disappear."

"Try me."

"The house is right here." He dismounted in a spot central to the four dominant features—the lake, the pine forest, Bear Mountain and the barn at the edge of the meadow. "It's made of lodgepole pine," he explained as he helped her down, having ground-tied his horse simply by dropping the reins. Her legs buckled when her boots hit the ground, but he steadied her, without laughing. One point for his good behavior, another for that of his horses now that the mare stood tethered without a stake. "We're standing in the living room. Dining room, kitchen. It's all open. Big double-sided fireplace right here." He gestured expansively and then specifically.

"A great room," Maggie enthused. "I love it. Such a communal feel. The colonials used it. The pioneers used it."

"Indians used it. I got this land from my white grandfather, but my Indian grandfathers lived here a lot longer."

"So you're doubly entitled."

"I don't know about that. This isn't reservation land, and it probably should be. I'm split down the middle." They turned toward the sound of hissing water. "Hey, Jaws, not in the kitchen."

"Where are the bedrooms?"

"There's one down here, along with a bathroom." He lifted his voice to the horse. "You hear that, ol' man?

And put the seat down when you're done. There are women around."

Maggie laughed. "You do your mama proud."

"Be sure and let her know." He raised his air sketching to the next level. "The master's upstairs, overlooking everything."

"As masters are wont to do."

"Until a mistress comes along."

She raised her brow. "You dream of a mistress?"

"Isn't that what the master's female partner is called?"

"These days that's what the married man's girlfriend is called. She has no place in a gentleman's fairy tale." She offered a pointed smile. "The kind of man who does his mama proud."

"That's up to her. A gentleman knows better than to tell a woman her place." His gesture said *after you.* "May I show you around outside? Watch your step." He flashed three long, tan fingers, and she took three mincing steps.

"My grandfather built that old barn."

"You're tearing it down?"

"Building it back up. Foundation's rock-solid, and the roof's held up pretty good. I'm saving what I can. Care to ride over and see my work?"

"I think I'll try walking over just to see if my legs still work." She nodded toward the horses. "How long will they stay?"

"Until they know I'm not looking." He took both sets of reins in hand again. The colt was already nursing noisily. "Guess we're all walking. Bring your baby, Oreo. I'll put you on grass."

The first few yards were painful, but the walk was

good for what was ailing her. The next ride would be easier, she told herself. And the next, and the next. Transformation from walker to rider might well be in the offing, much to the surprise of the woman who didn't like surprises. And there were more to come. A picnic plucked from his saddlebag, a climb she doubted she could make leading to a glorious view through the skeletal walls of the partly safe barn loft. They fed each other sandwiches and fruit, shared laughter, kisses, big dreams and a little history. Surprises and secrets had never sounded better.

"What happened to the house?" Maggie wondered. She was taking her time with the last of the grapes after he'd given the pretty-soon warning, his measure of daylight they had left rather than time. She was already feeling the pain of getting back in the saddle.

"It was a cabin," he said, gesturing toward a site closer to the barn than his dream house would be. "My great-grandfather started out raising sheep, but he gave it up when his wife died. Without her, he had to put all his eggs in one basket or the other, and he chose the store. He kept the land for my grandfather, who threatened to sell everything and move to Florida when Ma married an Indian. The story goes that the first time he saw me, he said he'd take grandchildren over gators any day."

"Children change everything," she said. "It's great when they bring out the best in people."

"And that's what happened. They became good friends, my white grandfather and my Indian father. I remember hearing them laugh together. It was a song. My dad had a low voice, and his laughter flowed smooth and easy. Grandpa's laugh was like the woodpecker to

Dad's mourning dove. Grandpa died when I was about Jimmy's age, and we lost Dad a few years later."

"The blood of two men from two worlds flows through you."

"Yep. Mixed blood, that's me."

"And the land is in good hands." She slipped hers over his.

"Mine and my brother, Zach's." He turned his palm to hers. "He's a good hand. Works hard, plays harder."

"Where is he?"

"Who knows? Rebel without a cause, that one. Used to be a hell of a rodeo cowboy, but I don't know what he's doin' now. Maybe he has a cause and we just don't know what it is." He squeezed her hand. "What's yours? You're a long way from home. There must be a cause."

"I'm certainly not a rebel," she said with a smile. "Jimmy, of course. He's my number-one cause. One A. Being a good nurse is one B. I envy the way you talk about family with such affectionate, lots of history. I can't recite much history. I moved around a lot growing up. My parents weren't close to their families, hence…"

She shook her head, choosing not to comment on the long-way-from-home part. Home would be nice. She'd go a long way *for* one. Maybe that was number one C.

"My mother is the one you should ask about causes. She lives for hers. She goes wherever nurses are needed the most. She's absolutely—" Maggie shook her head again "—amazing."

"Isolated rural towns, Indian country, hell, you don't have to go far to find people who need nurses." He smiled. "I'm glad you found us."

"I'm glad you found me. I like it here more all the time."

"Feel like you're home?"

"I want to be. My son really wants to be. So does your daughter."

"My mother's granddaughter. Merilee told her so." He drew away from her, reaching for the hat she'd taken off and placed atop the bag. "That much we know."

"All it would take is a paternity test." She watched him put his hat on, willed him to look up, see her, know that she was on his side. "I know you're not trying to get out of it, Sam. You'd never do that."

"She came looking for a place to hide. Somebody to take her in. She didn't know Ma, but she knew what kind of a woman she is from what I told her. She knew if she came here with a child in tow…"

"She knew you might be here," she insisted. "If not, all it would take would be a phone call from Hilda."

"I wish she'd left me something I could use against him besides…" He drew a deep breath, let it out slowly. "Merilee was running from Randone." Finally he met her gaze without hiding his fear. "Paternity testing could deliver Star into his hands."

"There's no chance?"

"You want details?" He shook his head, gave a mirthless chuckle. "There's a chance, but I gotta think his chances are a lot better."

She leaned close, slid her arm around his neck and rested her chin on his shoulder. *Strange wish for the man you love, Maggie—that he'd beat out another man in a paternity test that doesn't involve you.*

"How can I protect her?" he asked.

"She doesn't want to be with him." She leaned back, looked him in the eye. "That's obvious, Sam."

"Yeah, but I don't know exactly why. What he's done, what he might do, what he's after. And I can't push her. She's been through too much already." He braced his hand on his knee, preparing to stand. "Plus—I've gotta warn Ma—we can't be accused of coaching her or putting words in her mouth." He sighed on the ascent. "I don't know what he's up to, but if he gets himself a lawyer…"

"He says he just wants to be able to see her. Spend a little time with her."

"Is he spending time with you?" He offered his hand.

"I've run into him a few times." She looked up when the help she needed suddenly wasn't forthcoming. He'd turned to stone. "A *couple* of times."

"Merilee wasn't proof enough?" He yanked her to her feet. "Randone isn't somebody you wanna be runnin' into, Maggie."

"He can't do anything to me." She brushed her hands together—*just when she was getting comfortable with a man's surprises*—and squared her shoulders. "And I agree with you. He's up to something. He came here to get something besides Merilee. She's dead, and he's still here. That says something."

"He wants Star."

"But why? That's what we have to figure out before he—"

"Stay out of this, Maggie."

"I'm in it for Star. Sam, I really think he might show me his hand if he thinks—"

"Show you his *hand?* You keep thinkin' like that, Maggie, like it's a game with rivals and rules, and you're in for exactly the kind of surprise you say you don't like. Bad guys don't play by your rules."

He was looking down his aquiline nose at her, and it made her feel small. She wanted to grab him by the ear and pull his face down to her level.

"I'll take care of Star," he told her. "You've got your own kid to worry about. You watch yourself." He stepped back, as though she was crowding him. "If you're gonna be runnin' into Vic Randone, you damn well better watch yourself."

"Running into, yes, but also…" She gave him a second look. "What are you thinking, Sam?"

"I'm thinkin' it's gonna be a long ride back."

Chapter Eleven

Maggie had thought about it long and hard, and she'd made a plan. Discussing it with Sam was not an option. She'd explain once she had the goods. The means, the motive, the stuff of a good mystery, which she was pretty sure she had a better chance of solving than her dear lawman did. He couldn't see the forest for the ponderosa pines where Randone was concerned. Understandable, as long as he didn't entertain any wrong-headed idea that she was doing anything around his former friend *but* watching herself, as only a woman who'd experienced his kind of snakebite would know how to do.

She knew it wouldn't take much to hook Randone on his own fishing line. She'd hand over the missing piece to the Randone puzzle, and Sam would give her hell for going behind his back, but he'd do it in a nice way. And all would be well.

She'd laid a little more groundwork, running into Vic one more time outside the store. Not *technically* running into, since she wasn't planning to stop. She knew Hilda wasn't there. The Closed clock was hanging on the door, and there was Randone, trying the knob, putting up hand blinders and peeking through the glass, fiddling with the knob again. He wasn't looking for Star, and he probably wasn't looking for Hilda. The schedule for the end-of-the-year school programs had been printed in the weekly paper, and the second grade's was today.

What was he looking for?

Lucky was yapping like a magpie on the other side of the door. Nice distraction.

"If it's locked, she really means *closed.*"

He swung around, startled. "Oh, yeah. Hi, Maggie."

"Sometimes it says *closed,* but the door's open." She put on a no-harm-done smile. "Meaning, she's around here somewhere."

"I know. That's why I…" He closed the screen door, clearing his throat. "I've been around small towns. I know how these things work." He tucked his hands into the back pockets of his jeans. "I've hired a lawyer. I'll be going to court pretty soon."

"What are you asking for?"

"You know, I'm really not the hard-ass everybody takes me for. If they'd just let me spend some time with her, this wouldn't have to be a big battle. I'm not gonna be pushed out just because Sam wants to get back at me." He lifted one shoulder, tipping his head to the same side. "On the other hand, maybe I'm not what's best for Star. I don't know. But I have a right to hear it from Star. I deserve a little time with her, to see how she really feels about this. I don't want her to think I abandoned her."

"Then give it some time," Maggie suggested kindly.

"I don't have… I can't stay here indefinitely."

"You probably have a job to get back to."

"Well, sure."

"And the money you're expecting."

"The money? You know about…"

"You mentioned something about coming into a lot of money." She wrapped her arms around herself. "Which sounds interesting. Exciting. Gives me goose bumps."

"Money will do that."

"It's Merilee's money, isn't it?" She countered his guarded looked with the hint of a smile. "I was alone in the ambulance with her, remember."

"She was unconscious."

"More or less."

"And she said something about…"

"She mumbled something. 'Enough to take care of my baby.' I think that's what she said."

"I knew it." He lowered his head and moved closer. "Look, this isn't a good place to talk. I've got a room—"

"I'm not that kind of a girl, Vic." She touched his sleeve. "I'll meet you at the bar. The Man or Mare. I get off at eleven tonight."

"Where's Beaudry gonna be?"

"Playing with his horses or cleaning his gun. He's a cowboy, for heaven's sake." Maggie backed away smiling. "Like you said, I am not from around here."

She trailed her contaminated fingers over the porch railing as she took her leave. She couldn't wait to wash them.

* * *

Sam had missed Star's school program. He'd been working, knew he couldn't go, never said he would, didn't know why he felt like he'd *missed* something. But he did, and he was headed over to the store to make up for it—just bring yourself, said Ma—even though he'd had one hell of a day.

His conversation with tribal attorney Tom Ducheneaux had left him in limbo, a place he'd sworn off years ago. He wasn't sure where the word came from—some said it was somewhere between heaven and hell—but he pictured a fire-ravaged land, a dead tree, a charred limb with his heart hanging on it. Hell of a place to be.

Yes, Tom said, Sam could enroll his daughter, no test required. The Tribe didn't do DNA. They did lineage. You say she's your daughter, her mother says she's your daughter, she's your daughter.

What if some other guy says she's his daughter and wants to prove it?

The mother can refuse to have her tested.

Not if the mother's dead.

And the other guy's not Indian? Then we got a problem.

Tom had promised to do some research, but Sam could tell what he was thinking. Pay your money, take your chances. Living on both sides of the fence might look easy, but all too often you paid double for half the chance. And it was Star's chances he was gambling with.

He had to pick a good number before somebody made a bad move.

And not the kind that came flying for his head out in

front of the Emporium just as he was pocketing his keys. He grabbed the Frisbee out of the air, as deft a catch as he'd ever made, and went in search of the wild pitcher.

"Think fast!" Sam called out when he spotted two prime suspects running barefoot in the grass. They both leaped for the spinning disk, as did Lucky the Wonder Dog, but it kept sailing as all three crumpled to the ground.

"And it's a home run!" He whipped his hat off, tossed it in the air, snatched Jim up in one arm, Star in the other, and got tagged by their canine teammate, whose rule was the play didn't end until nobody moved. But it was okay if they all laughed.

They lay side by side in the grass, something Sam hadn't done in years, and watched pink sundown melt into purple twilight.

Sam tucked his hands behind his head. "Friday's your last day, huh? Baseball started yet?"

"I start Saturday," Star said.

"I missed the sign-up."

"Missed the sign-up?" Sam turned his head. "How did that happen?"

"Mom forgot to remind me. I hate it when she works three to eleven."

"Me, too," Star said. "I mean, I used to hate it."

"It's so cool to have your own store right downstairs. Your grandma gets to work right in her house," Jim said. "She's always home."

"And she's always at work." And the evening sky looked the same as it had when he was their age.

"And Sam has his office downstairs in his house.

Where we used to live we didn't know hardly anybody in our building." Star put her hand on Sam's arm. "I really like it here."

Sam gave a nod that nobody could see. "We'll get Jim signed up for baseball."

"I think it's too late," the boy said.

"Do you wanna play?"

"Sure."

"Then it's not too late. That's another good thing about Bear Root. Nobody's ever too late."

"There it is!" Star pointed, her small finger taking center stage in the big sky over Sam's world. "Star light, star bright, first star I see tonight—"

"I wish I may, I wish I might—" Jim joined in, making it a duet.

And then came the trio. "Have this wish I wish tonight."

Maggie met Randone at the Man or Mare. He was waiting in a booth, as instructed, leaving her the side with her back to the door. She wore a scarf on her head. She probably looked as ridiculous as she felt, but it was the kind of look that went unnoticed at the Man or Mare. Much of the saloon's clientele left their identity outside the door.

Randone got a laugh out of it. Said his grandmother had a scarf just like it. Putting her mark at ease was a scarf-wearing bonus. Maggie ordered a glass of wine— her choices were red or white—and meandered down to cases. Meandering seemed the best tack to take when cases were shrouded in fog.

"Was Merilee in pain, then?" he asked, fitting the bottom of his beer glass to the water ring on the table. "On the way to the hospital. Was she hurting?"

"It's hard to tell at that stage. My feeling is that when all else is failing, instincts prevail over mind and body. If that's true, then obviously Merilee cared about her child more than anything else."

"Enough to take care of my baby, she said." Still playing with the water ring, he smiled to himself. "That would be an understatement."

"How much is there?"

He was quiet for what seemed an eternity. *Damn.* Too soon, too direct. She'd blown it.

"Taking care of the kid's needs wouldn't even put a dent in it," he said finally. "I'm thinkin', set her up, you know, generously, and then you and me, we split seventy-thirty." He looked up, gold fever in his eyes. "You could live anywhere you wanted with thirty percent, and that's no lie."

"Thirty percent of what?"

"Sixty million."

Maggie nearly choked. *"Dollars?"*

"You want euros? Yen? Where do you wanna go, Maggie?"

Oh, God. Merilee had been trying to outrun some kind of criminal element. Mob boss. Drug kingpin. Arms dealer. And she was sitting across from the idiot trying to outsmart them. The idiot's idiot.

"I know she finally hit. I know it as sure as I'm lookin' at you. It hasn't been claimed yet, and it won't be unless I find the ticket in time."

Ticket?

"Okay, here's the deal. A palm reader once told Merilee to keep playing the same numbers in the Mega Bucks Lottery. She didn't say anything about the lottery, Merilee didn't, but somehow this Gypsy woman knew, and she told her to stick with this combination she had with ages and birthdays and all like that. She always had to buy the ticket on the same day of the week—Wednesday—and always the same numbers. I got to know the series by heart.

"So I haven't seen her in a while, and I'm watching the balls getting picked on TV, and it's Merilee's numbers. One after another. Bingo, bingo, bingo. And the ticket was purchased at her lucky SA. And the winner hasn't turned up yet? I mean, there is no doubt. I swear to God, if it's buried with her, I'm diggin' her up."

Laugh, Maggie. Can you laugh? You're not Nurse Maggie. You're Thirty-Percent Maggie.

She found a smile. The gleam in his eye said it was convincing enough to win her an acting award. It also hinted at a posthumous ceremony.

"Anyway, I go looking for her. Vanished. I find out where she moved, but nobody at the new place knows her. Of course the new school won't tell me anything, and the people at the old school, well, they don't like me much. I check out some of the stories she's told me over the years. Turns out her mother's dead, and her father's a drunk. Hell, you should've heard the fairy tales she spun for me about the father who was gonna kill me when she told him…whatever. So that's a dead end.

"And then it hits me. Sam Beaudry. Bear Root, Montana. I go online, and there's a Web page for the

Chamber of Commerce of Bear Root, and there's that country store he talked about. His mother runs it. Now, the last I heard, Sam was in the marines, but I see his mother's name listed, and I know Sam. Merilee does, too. Sam don't spin no fairy tales. His mother is the salt of the earth.

"So here I am."

The FBI's Most Wanted dropped off Maggie's mental top-ten threats list. She was down to two. Idiot, and idiot's idiot. Both were manageable.

"And what do you propose to do?"

"Find that ticket. You know she had it with her. If she signed it, I'll need Star. If she didn't, whoever wants the kid can have her."

"That's pretty cold."

"Wrong. It's generous. You help me find the ticket, we see what the score is, I'll cut you in. Best-case scenario, the ticket's unsigned. Hey, you never know with Merilee. She was an airhead. A junkie. If the ticket's signed, maybe we worry about paternity."

"What if Sam's the father?"

"Chances are he isn't. He's not gonna like those odds. One thing I know for sure about Sam, the kid's more important than the money." He studied her face. "Am I right?"

"I think so."

"You *know* so. Comes to that, we deal. Or I take my chances. I'm tellin' you, my chances are way better than his. That's why Merilee took off. And who would know better?"

"This sounds really crazy."

"Now you listen here." He moved his beer aside,

folded his hands on the table and leaned over them. "If you figure you've got it made either way, me or Sam, you think again. Sam finds out he's sharin' another woman with me, she'll get the outta-town-by-sundown routine. Don't let the door hit you in the ass on the way, he'll say." Vic reached across the table and slid the headscarf back. "And don't kid yourself. He *will* find out."

"I know nothing about a lottery ticket, Vic. All Merilee said was—"

"It's a piece of paper. It can be hidden anywhere. But you can be damn sure she brought it with her. And it isn't in the motel room. After I got the news, I made friends with Mama Crass. She let me move to Merilee's room so I could—" he waved his hands dramatically "—*feel* her spirit. I've checked every inch of that room. I've even listened to Mama Crass sing, if you can call it that, just to get her to talk. That ticket has to be hidden in something Merilee brought with her."

"What makes you think I'd go along with this? Or worry about what you might say to Sam?"

Vic smiled. "We all have our talents. Mine is judging character."

The light was on in Sam's office. Sure she was being watched, Maggie had gone home, waited a while and then hot-footed the four off-Main blocks to the old courthouse. She could see the back of Sam's head through Jimmy's favorite window, which was open.

"Sam!" Stage whisper. She felt a little silly, but the side door was locked. "I need to talk to you."

His chair swiveled slowly. She could see him, he

couldn't see her, but she was the one who looked ridiculous. He made sure she could tell by looking at him.

"Something wrong with your phone, Maggie?"

"I need to… I want to see you."

"You have the advantage."

"It's important. And I'd rather not go to the front door."

"You know what?" He shook his head as he pushed up from the chair. "I'm comin' over to your side. I don't like surprises, either."

"You might like this one."

He met her at the side door, and she followed him through dark storage spaces into bright, Sam-filled places—his desk, his coatrack, his lovely brown Stetson, his reception area, where he retrieved some paper and glanced at the multiline phone, presumably to see whether there were any lights on. He was a lawman. His work was important. She was either a silly girl or a crackpot sneaking around his window.

Finally he turned to her, arms folded, important papers in one hand, distant look in his eyes. "What's up?"

He knew more than he was letting on, but he was going to let her tell it her way.

Damned lawman.

"I did feel little silly out there." She offered a discomfited smile, just so he knew. "You're thinking, so that's where Jimmy gets his—"

"Your son's at home. *Your* home. I had him home at nine. He expected you home shortly after eleven. I'm sure he's asleep by now, but you might want to—"

"I know he's home." *How dare he suggest otherwise?* She folded her arms, unconsciously mimicking his stance. They stood shield-to-shield. "I've been there, looked in on him, checked in with Lila. We need to talk."

"I don't. I just said all I had to say."

We'll see, mister. "I know what Randone's after."

"Do you?" He turned away, tossing the important papers on the reception desk, exactly where they'd been. "He's not getting Star. Anybody else is a free agent."

"It's about money, just as we thought."

"*You* thought." He returned for a stare-down. "If that's all it is, tell him to bring me his deal."

"It's a lot of money." Why wasn't he getting this? "A *ton* of money."

"He was down at the bar tonight with somebody who was wearing a scarf." He reached for the silky tail of the flowered scarf loosely draped around her shoulders—the blasted toilet paper stuck to her shoe—and, oh, the smirk on his face, letting her know what a poor excuse she was for an agent. Never secret. Hardly free. "Bartender couldn't tell whether it was man or mare."

"Very funny."

"You see me laughin'?" He tipped his head to one side. "So he showed you his hand, and you came to tell me what it looks like. I'm not interested, Maggie." His smile chilled her. "I am no longer interested."

"Don't, Sam. I'm not Merilee."

"There's a little Merilee in all of us, honey, which is what keeps Randone right on truckin'." He gave a humorless chuckle. "Don't look at me like that. I said *truckin'.*"

"I don't believe you're this blind."

"I don't, either. I oughta be flyin' around at night catching mosquitoes."

"For someone who said all he had to say five minutes ago—"

"Longest five minutes of my life."

"All right." She drew a deep breath. "All right, Sam, I'm outta here. After I tell you—and maybe this isn't news to you, but just in case, since you're the law around here—that there's probably a winning lottery ticket hidden somewhere in Merilee's stuff." Was that a flicker of surprise in those cold, dark eyes? "Yes, according to Vic Randone. That's what he came for. It's worth sixty million dollars."

He stared.

And then he laughed. Not long, not hard, but he did laugh.

"He oughta take that one back to Hollywood. If he could sell it to you, he can probably get somebody there to buy it."

"You know what I'm going to do, Sam Beaudry?" For one thing, she was going to use the front door. "I'm going to tell your mother. She'll know how important this is, and *she'll* take it seriously."

Chapter Twelve

All right, so he was acting like a jackass. Perfect match for a woman begging to get herself kicked in the teeth. Not that he'd take his act that far. Maggie could beg all she wanted, but she'd get no kick out of him. A no-trick pony, a no-kick jackass—boring but safe. If she wanted kicks, she was in luck. The master kick-ster was in town, and he didn't act. Randone was the real deal.

Sam climbed into his patrol car and went after her. He could've walked, but the scene would've been damned undignified. And it could get ugly, right out there on Main. If his personal tribute to the humble jackass was what it would take to wake the woman up, he'd take the show on the road. But give him some shelter. A door to close, a window to roll up.

Maybe she thought she was doing him a favor by

waving a red cape around Randone. *Yoo-hoo, bully! What'cha up to, big guy?*

She wasn't. He'd asked her nicely. Told her plainly. He'd made absolute sense, and he couldn't believe she hadn't taken it to heart. *Lottery ticket, my ass.* Damn it, Maggie was smarter than that.

And there she was, walkin' down the street. Walkin' after midnight. Sure as hell, she was on her way to tell his mother on him.

"Hey. Maggie." Sam took his foot off the accelerator and let the car creep along the curb, matching her pace. He had to shout—it *felt* like shouting—across the passenger seat. "Hey, I'm sorry."

She didn't look his way, didn't stop, didn't spare a drop of mercy.

"For what?"

"What I said. That's what happens when I keep talkin' past nothin' to say. Would you get in the car?"

She stopped.

He tapped the brake.

She balled her fists and punched her hips.

He draped his forearm over the steering wheel.

"Are you arresting me?"

"Yeah."

"On what charge?"

"Lookin' for trouble." He made a valiant attempt to smile. "Dressing up for Halloween out of season. Impersonating Sherlock Holmes."

"I was wearing a scarf, not a…" She swept her hands over and above her shoulders, down and out. "Cloak and dagger."

"Hope that means you're unarmed." He reached across the seat and opened the door. "Get in."

She stood her ground.

"*Please* get in."

She wasn't moving.

"Listen, Maggie, I don't know who you were trying to fool, but put that crazy bar scene together with me crawlin' down the street after you, and this town'll be laughing behind my back for a month."

He didn't know what it was about that image that spoke to her, but she jerked on the door and got in.

"I wasn't trying to fool anyone, really. I never know where you might show up—which is fine, you know, it's your job—but I just didn't want you butting in on my…" She slid down in the seat, rested her head back and sighed as he accelerated. "All right, my little investigation. I thought what happened in the Man or Mare was supposed to stay in the Man or Mare. Did the bartender call you?"

"He wondered if we should contact Homeland Security."

She groaned. "You gotta be kidding me."

"I don't *gotta*." He signaled at the corner. "But I might be."

"Well I'm not, so don't turn here. I hope Hilda hasn't gone to bed." She laid her hand on his shoulder. "Seriously. I think I know where she hid the ticket."

"You believe Randone's bull."

"It's her legacy, Sam." She squeezed his shoulder and shook it as though she thought he was asleep. "The lottery ticket is Star's legacy."

Hilda hadn't gotten much sleep lately. She'd almost forgotten what it was like to be fully responsible for the needs of a child. It had been years, *years* since she'd gotten up in the morning thinking about wrapping her day around the kids. No matter what she planned, she had to see to them first. She'd grown into the role with her boys, dealing with the changes in tiny doses, one day at a time. Having them grow slowly was one of those blessings a person didn't appreciate until hindsight kicked in. Hilda could look back now and realize that babies were demanding, but their needs were simple and straightforward. Mama met those needs without a second thought. It started out relatively easy.

But soon they started thinking for themselves. It happened gradually, and you adjusted. Or not. You did your best. Or maybe not, but you did what you could at the time. The thing was, you had some time to grow. You found enough energy to keep yourself and a couple more bodies trucking along. You were young.

That was then, and this was now. Dropping a seven-year-old into a journey that was maybe three-quarters complete seemed to fly in the face of a perfectly good design.

So, what's going on here, God?

Hilda wasn't getting much sleep lately because Star wasn't sleeping well. And when a seven-year-old woke up crying, you couldn't nurse her back to sleep. As Grandma, Hilda was once removed from being in charge. She was glad to give what she could, but she couldn't take away, couldn't demystify or uncomplicate. A generation stood between Hilda and Star, a generation made up of a dead mother and a mystery father.

Scary.

It was enough to wake a little girl up at night. Enough

to throw an old gal into a maelstrom of the kind of worries she'd thought she was done with. Enough to bring young and old together when the dark was too deep and the air too heavy for sleep. And that was a comfort, which was enough to get them through until morning.

One day at a time, one night at a time. Two different things, Hilda reminded herself as she slipped from Star's room, having sung her to sleep for the second time, only a few hours apart. Fortunately, she knew lots of songs. Star didn't seem to mind that she could only sing one note. Lucky probably did, but he tolerated the singing in exchange for the privilege of giving aid and comfort and being allowed to stay behind and cuddle with his new favorite pack member.

"Only if you're quiet," Hilda reminded him.

Tiptoeing from room to room, she nearly shot out of her slippers when she glimpsed two heads from the back of the sofa. It was black hair with a hat crease sweetly touching honey-blond hair recently released from rubber-band security. *Déjà vu.* Kids making out on the couch after Ma was supposed to be asleep.

"Zach?"

"Sorry, Ma." Sam turned around first. "Just me."

Then Maggie, with a smile. "Us."

"Sam." Hilda laughed. "First time for everything."

"Not the first time I've nearly fallen asleep to 'Puff the Magic Dragon,' but it's been a while. Kinda late, isn't it?"

"That's what I was thinking." She tousled his hair as she passed the sofa, which separated the eat-in kitchen from the living room.

"I mean, for Star." He plowed his hand through the thick, dark hair he'd inherited from his father.

"It's a little early, actually. It's usually right around three in the morning."

"She wakes up?" Sam turned, honing in. "Bad dreams?"

"She's been through a lot. I wish we could tell her that man was gone. That would…" She came around the end of the sofa and saw Star's scrapbook on the pine coffee table, the pink-and-green cloth-bound neatly dismantled. "What are you doing?" Hilda gaped at the culprits. "Sam, that's all she has. *What* are you *doing?*"

"No big surprise. Randone's after money," Sam said. "He thinks Merilee had a winning lottery ticket. We think Merilee might have hidden something in this album. And that is a big surprise, seeing as how at least one of us was thinkin' pretty straight no more than an hour ago." He folded his pocketknife. "How crazy does this look, Ma?"

"This late at night, you expect crazy."

Crazy about each other, as any clear-minded person could see. All it took was a crisis to bring it out. Hilda smiled inside. Hadn't she known all along they were made for each other?

"Don't worry, Hilda. I'm sure I can fix this." Maggie slipped to the floor, opened the book and felt around the edges inside the cover. "So it's not under any of the pictures. It's not in the spine." She took a closer look. "This isn't the original end paper." She looked up at Hilda. "I hate to tear into it."

Star would hate it, too. "I'll put the teakettle on," Hilda said.

"How 'bout coffee?"

"You know where the pot is, son." Making her way around back of the sofa, Hilda patted him on the shoulder and then wagged a finger at Maggie. "Chasing some crazy dream is one thing, but you start waiting on them, it doesn't stop."

"She's going to steam this off, just like they did in… What was that mystery we read last month, Hilda?"

"*Steam Heat,* and keep your voices down." She pointed at the open book. "Bring it to the kitchen. If Star wakes up and catches us tearing into her *legacy* we're in trouble."

Hilda got the water boiling and carefully applied steam to paper. Sam and Maggie flanked her and watched, seemingly fascinated. Kitchen science, she thought. The kind of project you helped the kids with. Curiosity piqued, minds set, they'd already started it, and they were going to see it through one way or another. Somebody had something to prove, and Ma was in charge of damage control.

"You should join the book club," Maggie told Sam. "You never know what kind of tips you'll pick up."

"One Sherlock in the family is plenty. I'm lookin' at two. If I'm lucky."

Hilda peeled the end paper back. There, in all its chances-are glory, was a Mega Bucks Lottery ticket. Nobody touched it. Water kept boiling, steam kept rising, pot kept rattling, and the three of them stared at Merilee's buried treasure.

"Somebody could be very lucky," Hilda said quietly.

Sam took matters in hand. "Or somebody went to a lot of trouble for nothing," he projected, flipping the paper over in his palm.

"It isn't signed," said Maggie. "That's like carrying around sixty million dollars in cash."

What a ridiculous number. "After taxes, it's probably only worth…" Hilda tabulated in her head as though she had to make change. "Thirty million?"

"Who says?" Sam flipped the knob on the stove as though he were turning off more than just blue flame. "Aren't you getting ahead of yourselves? It's a piece of paper. Who says—"

"That's exactly what Randone said. It's a piece of paper. It could be hidden anywhere." Maggie laid her hand on Sam's back. "But you said it better, Sam."

"And you found it."

And her son, Hilda noticed, didn't sound particularly thrilled about the whole thing. Sam, the skeptic. Every family needed one. She removed the scrapbook to the kitchen table and busied herself assessing the damage.

"Which means we're way ahead of him," Maggie was saying. "We know what he wants, and he doesn't know we have it."

"*We* don't know we have anything but Vic's bull."

"Where's your computer, Hilda?"

"What computer? We're an old-fashioned country store."

Maggie joined Hilda at the table. "I thought you carried all goods."

"All goods available before about 1960. We don't have room for a lot of stuff nobody really needs."

"How about a phone?" Sam was reading the small print. "We've got a phone. Right, Ma?"

Hilda watched her son dial the 800 number printed

on the ticket. She felt a little dizzy. *Sixty million dollars.* Talk about crazy. The important thing was to get the scrapbook repaired before Star saw what they'd done to it. *Sixty million dollars.* Absurd. Real people didn't win the lottery. Not that Merilee Brown was real—she'd come and gone without opening her eyes—but Star was real. Star was Hilda's granddaughter, no matter what.

Sam put the phone on speaker, and punched numbers according to the menu instructions.

A robotic voice confirmed the winning number. *If you are a Mega Bucks winner, press one for instructions. To hear the numbers again, press two.*

They looked at each other, stunned. No fist pumping, no cheers. Star could be rich. And Vic Randone—who very much wanted to be rich—might be…*could very well be* her father.

Sam pressed for instructions. Sign the ticket in ink. Download a claim form from the Web site. Fill it out and make copies of everything. *The original ticket is your only receipt.*

"Let the wild rumpus begin," Sam muttered as he slowly hung up the phone. He looked up at two puzzled women. "*Where the Wild Things Are.* She read it to me the other night. She's a good reader."

"Now she can buy herself a whole library," Maggie said.

"You heard the part about being eighteen or older."

"You're her father. You know it, and she knows it. You don't need a blood test. I'll bet she's never read a book to Randone." Maggie rose from the chair she'd occupied for about thirty seconds and stood by her man.

"The court won't let him take her, Sam. All he wants is the money."

"Let him have it." He tossed the ticket on the table. "I mean it. He'll choke on it. He'll blow himself up with it. Let him have the damn ticket."

"What about Star?" Maggie glanced at Hilda—*Is he serious?*—and back at Sam. "That's a lot of money, Sam, and it should be hers."

He stared at the ticket, lying inoffensively on the table.

"He'll demand paternity testing. I'll fight him, and he'll have lawyers taking his case on contingency because there's a big pot of gold at stake," he reeled off as though he were reading tea leaves. "If he's her biological father, she'll never be rid of him. Look what happened to her mother." He turned to Maggie. "Damn, this is just like that old riddle. You're in a rowboat, and you've got a gunnysack full of money, a vulture and a little girl."

"That's easy. You…" Maggie's face went from easy to not-so-much as she followed the course of Sam's direction. He grabbed a pen from Hilda's telephone caddy, turned back to the table and planted his left thumb on the ticket.

"What are you doing?" the women demanded in unison.

"Giving it to somebody we can trust." Sam pushed the pen into Maggie's hand.

"No." She jerked her hand back, seemingly scorched. The pen clattered on the linoleum floor. "No!"

"I turn it in, he goes after Star. We don't have anything he wants, he leaves us alone." Sam straightened, his hand coming away from the ticket, eyes on Maggie.

"He can't touch you, Maggie. You've got a conscience, you'll let it be your guide. You can go anywhere, do anything you want, no problem. You know, just quietly set something aside for Star."

Hilda held her breath. An absurd amount of money was…an absurd amount of *money*.

"Sam, this isn't right," Maggie said quietly. "This *really* isn't fair."

Hilda breathed.

"You'll do the right thing, Maggie. And he'll go away, and I won't have to spend the rest of my life in prison for killin' him."

Glances were exchanged all around before two out of three laughed.

Serious Sam missed the humor. His sigh sounded painful. Hilda wanted to hug him, but she couldn't, of course. This was his to play out, and nobody could handle it better. She truly believed that, and a mother's bias had nothing, *almost* nothing to do with it. Thank God all she had to do was mend Star's photo album.

"I don't know what to do," Sam admitted. "Kinda makes me sick. Nobody needs this much money. But it's rightfully hers."

"You'd really put my name on that?"

"In a heartbeat."

"Did I *say* the right thing? What time was it when you started trusting me?"

"That wasn't your problem tonight, Maggie. That was all mine. Baggage, remember?"

"He can be bought, Sam. I think that's a better option. Offer him a share, but only if he stays out of Star's life. Start the adoption procedure. It shouldn't take long as long as he stays out of it. He gets his share when the adoption is final."

Good plan, Hilda thought as she experimented with tucking the pink-and-green cloth back into place. Maggie was a good planner.

"Can't trust him," Sam said. "If he had the ticket, he'd be gone. He'd never look back."

"Merilee gave her life to bring Star and that ticket here, to you."

"You think she came here to die?"

"I think she came here for help. And I think the 'legacy' is rightfully Star's."

"Damn." Sam touched the ticket with a wary forefinger. "If she could only have one or the other, would she take the sixty million, or would she become a Beaudry? Right now she just wants to be safe, but what about ten years from now, when she finds out she could have had…" Sam exchanged glances with Hilda. Back to Maggie, but softly now. Seriously. This was Sam, sticking his neck out. "What would you pick?"

Hilda removed the scrapbook and herself to the kitchen counter, screening herself behind a suspended cupboard. She opened the cupboard door, thinking *glue,* telepathing *you.*

"I've already rejected the sixty million," Maggie reminded him.

"I don't handle rejection well. Proposals, either, for that matter."

"Is there something in this for me? Because it's all sounding rather hypothetical."

"Marriage," he said. "To me. How does that sound?"

Hilda did a totally silent one-handed air chin-up.

"Complicated," Maggie said.

"Yep. So I've heard. Risky proposition, marriage. If sixty million doesn't cut it—"

"I'd claim it if it were mine to claim. But it's Star's. And *you are her*—"

"How about love? It's pretty simple, coming from me. It's real, and it's true, and it's mine to give. And it's yours to claim."

"It would be a package deal. Love me, love my child."

"Back at'cha. With any luck."

"I don't believe in luck, Sam. But I believe in you. I'll take you over a pile of money any day."

From the bedroom came a small, frightened voice. "Grandma?"

"Get this out of here," Hilda hissed, snatching the trashed scrapbook off the counter and shoving it into Maggie's hands. "Take it all outside." *Have yourselves some privacy.* She shooed them toward the door to the deck, and she intercepted Star with open arms and soothing words.

He kissed her as soon as they got outside. He grabbed her and kissed her, and she clutched the scrapbook in one arm, snaked the other around his neck and opened herself, every cell, every pore, drawing him in through his powerful, yea-saying kiss.

"You mean it?" he whispered, and then he kissed her again, and when he finally let her breathe, all she could do was nod. So he kissed her again.

They sat together on the glider, holding each other. They were short on answers, long on feelings, and those were huge. Scrapbook aside on the seat next to her, fate aside, fortune aside, they steepled their fingertips together, her hand stretching to match his before they collapsed them together, fingers interlocked.

But when she shifted against his shoulder, the scrapbook nudged her hip.

"I think people usually hook up with a lawyer right away, Sam," she said, thinking out loud. "Do you know a good one?"

"Seems like getting lawyered up first would kinda take the romance out of the wedding." He gave her an opening, but she let it slide. "Okay, the custody thing."

"I'm thinkin' on the lottery ticket thing." She'd meant for it to sound breezy, but she hadn't quite pulled it off. Cold was probably how it sounded. But the ticket had to be signed. "Please don't think I'm being…but you always see winners showing up in the news with their attorneys. I guess you'll need another one for the custody issue."

"Great." He gave her a shoulders a reassuring squeeze. "That's the part of my job I could do without. Lawyers."

"Randone says he's in touch with legal counsel."

"Sure, he is."

"Sure, he is," echoed Randone.

Chapter Thirteen

"Sounds like you found it."

He was standing at the top of the landing, and he was holding a gun. Maggie's first outrageous thought was *Where did he come from?* The depths of hell, obviously. But shouldn't there have been some warning? A creaking step? The smell of sulphur? A barking dog at the very least?

Okay, key point: he was holding a gun. Maggie wanted to crawl under Sam's arm, but sitting up might have made better sense. Sam needed his arm.

"You've picked yourself a winner this time, Sam. This one's predictable. I told her what I was looking for, and she went right out and found it."

Maggie squared her shoulders. This was where he would say, *Hold it right there.*

But he moved to the side of the glider. Her side, Sam's weak side.

"I thought it would take a little longer, Maggie. You're good. Only, I'm a little disappointed that you stopped off to tell Sam. That makes you a little too good." He smiled. His teeth were blue-white in the moonlight. "I like 'em good at going after what they want, what I want—hell, what everybody wants—but, you know, not *too* good."

"If you'd just given me a few more minutes, I would have had the ticket, Vic."

"Right. Lawyers, custody, even a wedding in the works."

"And how else would I get the ticket, Vic?" She wasn't sure where this act was coming from or how long she could keep the shivering creepies out of her voice, but with the better part of her brain suddenly anesthetized, she had to use what she had.

Auto mouth.

"I thought it might take a little longer, too, but you were right about Sam. He wants Star, free and clear. I want the thirty percent you mentioned. I don't see why the three of us can't come to some kind of an agreement."

"There's four of us. You two and us two." Randone's gun hand betrayed a twitch. "I wonder which pair has more clout."

"That depends on whose name is on the ticket."

"Maggie," Sam warned.

But she was getting into character. "We can always add another name."

"We can always add two or three more to your side there. Who's in the house? You wanna bring 'em on out?" Vic chuckled. "I like my side just fine, but you guys can bring in kids, old ladies, dogs, whatever. Seems like you'd wanna keep them out of it, but, hey…" His smile faded, face went dark. "It's like this. If Merilee signed the ticket, then I'm Star's daddy. We're a happy little family. Now where is it?"

"Maggie, go inside and get him the ticket," Sam said calmly. "He doesn't want Star. He wants the money."

"He could still—"

"Maggie, the man is pointing a gun at you. I want you to go inside and get the ticket."

"What's to stop him from—"

"Me." And the arrows flying out of his eyes. "I'll stop him from taking anything else." He touched her arm. "You made a choice, Maggie. You said you didn't want your name on that ticket."

"I don't. But once he has it…" They'd have no leverage, right? "Don't you understand, Vic? That poor woman paid the ultimate price."

"And the ticket is his price, Maggie."

"What's yours?" Vic asked her. "Do you wanna come with me? Is your name on the ticket?"

Maggie started up from the glider.

"Wait a minute," Vic said. "Where's the ticket?"

"It's right inside. Kitchen table."

Vic waved her back down on the glider with the point of his gun. "Let's let Sam get the ticket."

"Vic, we can keep this real simple," Sam said, leaning slightly, trying to put himself between the gun and Maggie. "You take the damn ticket, you let us keep Star. Maggie can get—"

Randone placed the barrel of the gun two inches from Maggie's head.

"Get it, Sam."

Sam eased himself off the glider and backed toward the door.

"Turn the lights on first thing so I can see what you're doing."

"I don't care about the ticket, Vic. Believe it, and be careful with that."

"Sure." Vic waved Sam inside, and the light came on instantly. "Don't move," Vic told Maggie as he backed off, gun out of her reach. He watched through the window. "Don't wake anyone up. Don't touch anything but that…yeah. That's gotta be it."

Vic pulled Maggie off the glider, stood behind her and put his arm around her shoulders. "Bring it out here, Sam."

Maggie concentrated on the sound of Sam's boot heels. Easy, steady, sure. The thing touching the back of her head couldn't hurt her. Not with Sam Beaudry coming this way.

The arm tightened. "Sam, you'll be walkin' down to my car ahead of us. I'm down the hill there on the side street. You'll wanna go down these steps the way I came up—along the inside, where they don't squeak."

They became a little backyard procession, the gun now lodged against the small of Maggie's back, Vic's step becoming almost buoyant. "Man, this town is dead," he said quietly. "No traffic, nobody on the streets this time of night, nuthin'."

When they reached the small brown beater, Sam was directed to the passenger's side, while Vic sandwiched

Maggie between himself and the hood of the car. He'd left the windows down, and he told Sam to reach inside and get a flashlight out of the glove box. "We really should take his car, huh?" he said to Maggie. "It's sittin' right out in front of the store. I've always wanted to drive one of those."

"We?" Maggie watched Sam pull up from the window, flashlight in hand. He wasn't looking at her, wasn't saying anything, just waiting. "Use your head, Vic. All Sam wants is Star. He just handed you a lottery ticket worth sixty million dollars. All you have to do is go away. Sign the ticket and claim the money. Do you really want to steal a car and take a hostage?"

"Well, I do have to get outta town by sunrise." Vic chuckled. "Stay on that side, Sam. You notice I'm stayin' out of his reach. He could blow anytime. I know this guy. I know him well."

"You don't have to worry about his reach as long as you don't take anything but the money," Maggie said.

"Yeah, you're probably right. You're probably right." He grabbed the back of her hair. "I don't wanna hurt you, so put your hands flat on the hood." He pushed her head down between her hands and pressed the barrel of the pistol to her temple. "Now, Sam, I wanna see that ticket flat on the hood. Slide it across with one hand and shine some light on the matter. I just wanna make sure."

Maggie held her breath and watched the paper slide into her view. Sam's fingers. Sam's knuckles. Sam's wrist, watch, cuff folded back, all Sam. Steady, slow, sure.

"Don't make me nervous, Sam."

Sam did nothing to *make* him. He just was. Maggie could feel it in the cold thing that touched her temple.

The light went on, and the ticket shone bright.

"Ahh, that looks beautiful. Turn it over. Good." He snatched it off the car hood and rubbed it between his fingers. "Feels about right. I think Vic's got himself a winner.

"Slide your keys over here, Sam. The keys to your fuzzmobile."

Metal slid against metal and then chinked as Vic pocketed the keys. He jerked Maggie up by the hair and opened the driver's door on the beater. "I hope you know how to drive, Maggie. These roads are pretty treacherous at night."

She got a fleeting glimpse of Sam, connected with his eyes. There was something there for her. Anger, fear, love, assurance—all Sam. Every big, beautiful, blessed bit of Sam.

"Now you're makin' a mistake, Vic."

"This is a drive-through town. You've got one highway, so I can't exactly lose you, man. All I want is a head start. Keep your eyes open when you come after me. I'll let her off when she gets to be a nuisance."

"Kidnapping is a serious—"

"We're just taking a ride," Vic said as he climbed into the car and pulled Maggie in after him. "I don't want any trouble, Sam. You had my lottery ticket—mine and Merilee's. I got it back from you. That's all there is to it." He shoved his keys into the ignition. "Oh, and you got your kid. The one you didn't know about. No hard feelings, right? Everybody's happy."

* * *

Sam wasted no time getting hold of Della, who was manning the desk and reported that Phoebe was on her way back from Bear Mountain. He gave her the rundown on Randone and told her to call his deputies in Medicine Hat for backup. He asked her to let him know who was available and where they were coming from, have a set of keys ready to hand off to him when he got there in his mother's van, and get him Phoebe's 10-20—an update on her location. There was a 207 in progress.

"Kidnapping? Who's been kidnapped?"

Unauthorized question. How many times had he told her identity wasn't an issue?

"Maggie Whiteside."

"Holy moly, Sam. How did—"

"Don't ask. Out the door with a spare set of keys, Della. I'm almost there."

He took the handoff on the keys and ordered a 10-24 as he rolled past her on his drive-through—car-to-car transmit with Phoebe—plus a no-bull 11-99—officer needs help. Any other time he might have joked, something like "Supersize me." He would think about other times and other calls later. Right now he was enough of a joke, having been stripped of his keys. By the time Sam barreled the length of Main in his beefed-up patrol car, Radone had his head start.

Phoebe's call came moments later, and without official preface. "Sam? Sam, I had him."

"What do you mean *had?*" Sam turned his flashers on as he swung around a tight curve.

"It had to be him. I blocked the road, and he tried to get around me. He took the plunge."

"Plunge?"

"The hairpin at the four-mile. He went over. I heard him bounce off the rock face at least three times. Even if he was alive—which he's not—we couldn't get to him."

Sam went numb. He slowed for the curve approaching the cemetery, his mind flickering in blue and red—no images, just colors rolling like an old-fashioned TV on the blink—and robotically echoing *alive,* not, *alive,* not.

Up ahead something moved.

Deer?

Flag. Flying, fluttering, hand, arm, face lit up like sunshine. It was a scarf. It was a woman.

It was Maggie.

He had her in his arms before his brain caught up to his body. Brake, park, door, run—no thought. No question. She was real, and she was there, and she was whole.

He said nothing. His throat burned, his gut churned. Not sick, just crazy scared. He felt her hair between his fingers and her warm breath against his neck hissing the *S,* her lips brushing his skin on the *m.* His name. He felt it, heard it, and she'd said it. His name. Walking, talking, holding, hugging, living, breathing Maggie. He took her face in his hands and wiped her tears with his thumbs. Her eyes glittered—blue, red, blue, red—and she touched his cheek with a trembling hand. Tears he didn't know he had.

"He let me go, Sam."

"You okay?" He smoothed her hair back, searched her face. "You're not hurt?"

"He let me go."

"He went off the road. Phoebe saw...called." He was afraid to look away from her face, even for a second. "He drove off...plunged..." His throat went dry. He swallowed. "I know the road. I know that drop."

"I'm fine. He let me go." She put her arms around him, held tight, lay her head on his chest. "I'm fine."

"Jeeze."

"I'm sorry, Sam. I was trying to help." She tipped her head back and smiled through her tears. "Don't know when to keep my mouth shut."

"That's what I like about you, Maggie."

"What?"

"Everything." He kissed her. "Every...blessed... thing."

Randone's car was visible the next day, hung up in a chasm, landed on its back like a turtle with a caved shell. Through his binoculars Sam could see an arm. A hand. Wouldn't be there long. The vultures circling overhead didn't need binoculars. It wasn't the first car the mountain had claimed. Usually they were kids, drunks, or tourists.

Vic had known better. He'd been no stranger to Rocky Mountain roads. Sam knew that for a fact. They'd been friends once, knocking around the countryside, hiring on wherever anybody was drilling. Vic hadn't been hard to live with back then. But circumstances changed, and it was people who changed them.

Somewhere at the bottom of the cliff—maybe inside the car or hung up in the scrub pines below—there was a piece of paper printed with a series of numbers that could certainly change circumstances. And people. Sam wondered how it might have changed Star's circumstances, whether it would have changed Star. Her name would not have been on the ticket. Whose, then? And who would that person have become? Big money could do strange things to people. Or so Sam had heard. The very prospect had changed Vic Randone once and for all.

One thing was certain—that car was Vic's tomb. There was no way to move the damn thing, and Sam purely regretted that. Not that he wanted to go prospecting for paper. Not that he particularly felt like burying Vic. But he hated the thought that Bear Mountain had to suffer the indignity of another junk car rusting in plain view. They were no deterrent for local would-be NASCAR drivers, immortal at sixteen, and Sam needed no reminder that some mishaps just would not be headed off, no matter how hard he tried. Every one of them saddened him.

Every single one.

He drove past the old courthouse with the upstairs apartment that would have to serve more than just him for a while, past the school that was closed for the summer, past the church where he figured to arrange a wedding soon. He pulled over in front of Allgood's Emporium, glanced down the street at the Mountain Mama Motel sign. A lot had happened lately, but you wouldn't know it looking at Bear Root. From one end of Main to the other, Sam's hometown hadn't changed much since he was a kid.

And now, suddenly, he *had* a kid. Soon he'd have two. He laughed as he jumped over the two plank steps and landed on the porch—hadn't done that in a while—giving himself all the credit he deserved for wasting no time.

Star met him at the door. She was all dressed in her boots and jeans, long-sleeved T-shirt with glittery stars all over it. Pure Montana cowgirl.

"Can't Grandma go with us?"

"We're picking up Maggie and Jim. We've only got the two saddle horses right now, but it won't be long before we can have more."

"Grandma doesn't ride horses," Hilda said as she stepped onto the porch. "See these flat-heeled boots? They're made for walkin'. So don't be gettin' any more horses on my account. Noticed Maggie was pretty miserable after you took her out there the other day."

Sam adjusted his hat. "Is that what she said?"

"I know saddle misery when I see it. What she said was..." His mother shifted into high voice. "'Sam showed me his dream house.'"

"You wanna see it, too?" he asked Star, hoping he wouldn't be hearing any such mockery coming out of her little mouth anytime soon. Had to be careful what you said around kids. Had Ma forgotten? "You have to use your imagination. It's not built yet. But I'm gonna finish some fencing this summer so we can get two more saddle horses. One for each member of the family, so we don't have to double up. Grandma gets the colt. She can teach him some tricks. Soon as I finish the barn, I'll get started on the house. So today we're gonna show you and Jim where it's gonna be. I hope you like it. I'll get it done a lot faster if I know you and Jim and Maggie are gonna be living there with me."

"What about Grandma?"

"I'm not moving out to the country until I retire," Hilda said. "After my grandchildren take over the store. Coulda' done it sooner, but the storekeeper's blood skipped a generation. Now, Star…"

"I can already take care of the store, Sam. I can stock canned goods and bag groceries."

"You can write your own ticket, honey. Now, I've got something I need to tell you about." Soon as he got this out of the way, maybe he'd start working on getting her to call him *Dad.* He took her hand as he seated himself on the porch bench. "There was a bad accident on Bear Mountain last night, and Vic Randone was…he was killed." She didn't move. As far as he could tell she was studying their hands clasped together on his knee. "You okay?"

Without looking up, she nodded.

"Okay. We've got the whole day, and we're put—"

"Are they going to put him near my mother?" she asked quickly.

"Um…his car crashed on the side of the mountain. I don't know if—"

"I just don't want him in her same graveyard." She looked up, wide-eyed. "Put him somewhere else, okay?"

"I'll see to it."

"And could we go there today? I wanna take her some flowers."

"Sure."

"And I wanna tell her everything's gonna be okay."

Sam smiled. "We can do that right now."

In the Bear Root cemetery a breeze rustled the meadow grass, fast recovering from its Memorial Day mowing.

It was not a manicured burial place. Ashes to ashes, dust to dust, and grass to grass was the Bear Root mourner's prayer. The newest grave was already beginning to sprout. Its temporary marker would be replaced with a granite memorial, but for now there was a small stake holding up a metal placard. Trapped between the framed name and dates and the red earth was a dried flower.

And then came a scrap of paper. It drifted down directly, as though the breeze had found its target, and lodged between the flower and the nameplate. Just a piece of paper with numbers printed on it, one of which could also be found on the marker. Lucky numbers on a piece of paper.

It could have been hidden anywhere.

* * * * *

Mills & Boon® Special Moments™
brings you a sneak preview.

In Their Second-Chance Child *Tony Herrera must have
been crazy to hire his ex-wife Rebecca to oversee his
vocational bakery for foster kids! But Becca was best
for the job…and his four-year-old daughter fell for
Becca instantly. Were Tony and Becca heading down
the road to renewed heartache or was this the
second chance they never dreamed possible?*

*Turn the page for a peek at this fantastic new story
from Karen Sandler, available next month in
Mills & Boon® Special Moments™!*

*Don't forget you can still find all your favourite
Superromance and Special Edition stories
every month in Special Moments™!*

Their Second-Chance Child
by Karen Sandler

Rebecca had anticipated a difficult reunion with Tony. She'd expected that storm cloud of anger in his face, the hardness in his usually soft brown eyes. As much as she wished otherwise, she'd come here knowing she might be escorted from the property the moment Tony realized that Rebecca Tipton was actually Becca Stiles.

But she hadn't been prepared for the heat that sizzled inside her, the throbbing low in her body. It had been more than eleven years since they'd last made love, since they'd been man and wife, but her body remembered his touch, his scent, every intimate word whispered in her ear.

His dark brown hair was shorter, but just as thick. His shoulders were broader, almost too wide for the Hawaiian shirt he wore, his arms more muscular. His hands were the same, blunt-fingered and strong, but like everything else about him, they spoke of power and competence. During their marriage, their lives had been filled with unknowns. Now it looked as if he'd found some answers.

As she gazed up at him, he leaned toward her, still angry but maybe pulled by the same memories. He almost reached for her; she could see his fingertips stretching toward her. Then he strode past her and put his desk between them.

"Sit," he said sharply, then bit out, "please."

Was he going to give her a hearing after all? Rebecca lowered herself back into the secondhand office chair.

"You remarried," he said.

"I hear you did as well."

Something dark flickered in his face. "I can't possibly offer you this position."

Rebecca dug in. "You know as well as I do that I'm perfect for the job."

"You're married. This is a live-in position, and I don't have accommodations for a couple."

"I'm divorced."

A long, silent beat as he took that in. Then his gaze narrowed on her. "Estelle didn't say a word when she recommended you."

"You wouldn't have even considered me if you knew. Even if no one else with my qualifications has applied."

"I may have named the program after Estelle, but she isn't the one that hires and fires here. I am." His gaze fixed on her, his dark eyes opaque.

She shivered, blaming the chill fingering down her spine on the gust of cool air spit out by the window air conditioner. Wrapping her arms around herself in self-defense, she considered the arguments she'd prepared, knowing in advance she'd have to fight for this job.

But did she really want to? Maybe he was right—she ought to return to her car. Head back down Highway 50, don those same imaginary blinders she'd worn on her way here as she passed the off-ramp to West Hills Cemetery. Take Interstate 5 south and drive back down to L.A.

Except what waited for her there was just more despair. In the two months since Rebecca's foster daughter, Vanessa, had been returned to her mother, Rebecca had been hollowed out with grief. One moment social services was dotting the i's and crossing the t's on Rebecca's adoption of Vanessa, the next they were calling to notify her that Vanessa's mother had regained custody. Now the five-year-old girl was lost to Rebecca forever. Just as her son was.

She had to at least plead her case with Tony. Hands linked in her lap, she tipped up her chin in challenge.

"You won't find anyone to match what I can offer. You

know from my résumé I have impeccable credentials as a baker. I've volunteered teaching cooking classes for two years at a local Boys and Girls Club. And you know as well as I do that my understanding of what these kids have been through in the foster system isn't just academic."

She'd spent a year in foster care when her parents were badly injured in a freak accident and required extensive rehab to get back on their feet. Estelle had lavished loving care on the frightened nine-year-old that Rebecca had been, becoming a second mother to her in that short time.

Tony's hands curled around the arms of his chair, the skin over his knuckles taut. "You'd be living here full-time. We'd be in each other's faces practically twenty-four/seven."

"It's been eleven years. We can put the past behind us."

"Some pasts shouldn't be forgotten."

That stung, although she probably deserved it. "I know I'd do a good job."

He almost seemed to consider it, then shook his head. "I have to think of the kids. They've all just been emancipated from foster care, and they're anxious enough about their futures. I can't increase their tension by adding you into the mix."

"Don't you think I deserve a chance?"

He shoved his chair back and pushed to his feet. "Damn it, Becca, these kids need some constancy in their lives. They need someone who will commit their heart and soul to them for the entire five months of the session. I can't let you get involved with them and then have you leave them in the lurch if the going gets tough."

He might as well have punched her in the gut. "I was nineteen years old, Tony. Young and confused. I'm not about to walk out on these kids the way I…"

The way I walked out on you. The silent words seemed to echo in the small space. On their heels came the harsher indictment—*The way I walked away from our lost son.*

He started past her, moving toward the door. Rising, she put her hand on his arm to stop him.

A mistake. Her palm fell on his biceps, just below where the wildly colored sleeve of his shirt ended. His skin was hot, the musculature under it rock hard. She yearned to move her hand along the length of his arm, from biceps to forearm to wrist, then lock her fingers in his.

His dark gaze burned into her, the visual connection sending a honeyed warmth through her. Her heart thundered in her ears, so loud she thought he must hear it, would know her self-control was slipping away.

Then he covered her hand with his. To break the contact, she thought, to get free of her. But his fingers lingered, his thumb stroking lightly across the back of her hand.

He pulled his hand back with a jolt, putting space between them at the same time. "You should go." His voice scraped across her nerves like rough silk.

SPECIAL MOMENTS™ 2-in-1

Coming next month

THE TYCOON'S PERFECT MATCH by Christine Wenger

Brian Hawkins and Mari had loved each other – until a misunderstanding tore them apart. Now that Mari was back in town, would all the old feelings come back?

THEIR SECOND-CHANCE CHILD by Karen Sandler

Tony must have been crazy to hire his ex-wife Rebecca! But Becca was best for the job…and his four-year-old daughter adored her. Was this their second chance at love?

A MARRIAGE-MINDED MAN by Karen Templeton

Lasting relationships had never been in the cards for single mum Tess Montaya. But when her teenage sweetheart re-entered her life, it looked as if this time they were playing for keeps.

FROM FRIEND TO FATHER by Tracy Wolff

Now things have changed, Reece and Sarah have to be parents – together. Fine. Easy. But only if Reece can control his attraction to Sarah.

AN IMPERFECT MATCH by Kimberly Van Meter

Dean had to give Annabelle a job – he always helps a damsel in distress. But the boss is having a hard time keeping his distance from the gorgeous single mum.

NEXT COMES LOVE by Helen Brenna

From the moment Erica steps off the ferry, Sheriff Garrett Taylor can't fight the attraction igniting between them – even though trouble is following her!

On sale 21st May 2010

Available at WHSmith, Tesco, ASDA, Eason and all good bookshops.
For full Mills & Boon range including eBooks visit
www.millsandboon.co.uk

SPECIAL MOMENTS™

Single titles coming next month

A BRAVO'S HONOUR
by Christine Rimmer

For more than a century, ranch families the Bravos and Cabreras have feuded. Then Mercy Cabrera falls for Luke Bravo, and their forbidden love tests the limits of a Bravo's honour.

LONE STAR DADDY
by Stella Bagwell

Ranger Jonas Redman thought he had his assignment under control – until the ranch's very single, very pregnant heiress captured his attention and wouldn't let go…

CLAIMING THE RANCHER'S HEART
by Cindy Kirk

Stacie had a knack for matchmaking, except for herself! Being matched with Josh must have been a computer error – or was this rugged rancher really her perfect man?

TO SAVE A FAMILY
by Anna DeStefano

When her latest case involves a single mother with three kids, Emma is determined to see justice done. But falling for Lieutenant Rick Downing wasn't part of the plan…

On sale 21st May 2010

Available at WHSmith, Tesco, ASDA, Eason and all good bookshops.
For full Mills & Boon range including eBooks visit
www.millsandboon.co.uk

millsandboon.co.uk Community

Join Us!

The Community is the perfect place to meet and chat to kindred spirits who love books and reading as much as you do, but it's also the place to:

- **Get the inside scoop from authors about their latest books**
- **Learn how to write a romance book with advice from our editors**
- **Help us to continue publishing the best in women's fiction**
- **Share your thoughts on the books we publish**
- **Befriend other users**

Forums: Interact with each other as well as authors, editors and a whole host of other users worldwide.

Blogs: Every registered community member has their own blog to tell the world what they're up to and what's on their mind.

Book Challenge: We're aiming to read 5,000 books and have joined forces with The Reading Agency in our inaugural Book Challenge.

Profile Page: Showcase yourself and keep a record of your recent community activity.

Social Networking: We've added buttons at the end of every post to share via digg, Facebook, Google, Yahoo, technorati and de.licio.us.

www.millsandboon.co.uk

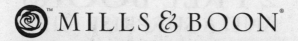

2 FREE BOOKS
AND A SURPRISE GIFT

We would like to take this opportunity to thank you for reading this Mills & Boon® book by offering you the chance to take TWO more specially selected books from the Special Moments™ series absolutely FREE! We're also making this offer to introduce you to the benefits of the Mills & Boon® Book Club™—

- **FREE home delivery**
- **FREE gifts and competitions**
- **FREE monthly Newsletter**
- **Exclusive Mills & Boon Book Club offers**
- **Books available before they're in the shops**

Accepting these FREE books and gift places you under no obligation to buy, you may cancel at any time, even after receiving your free books. Simply complete your details below and return the entire page to the address below. You don't even need a stamp!

YES Please send me 2 free Special Moments books and a surprise gift. I understand that unless you hear from me, I will receive 5 superb new stories every month, including a 2-in-1 book priced at £4.99 and three single books priced at £3.19 each, postage and packing free. I am under no obligation to purchase any books and may cancel my subscription at any time. The free books and gift will be mine to keep in any case.

Ms/Mrs/Miss/Mr _____ Initials _____

_____

Surname _____

Address _____

_____

_____ Postcode _____

E-mail _____

Send this whole page to: Mills & Boon Book Club, Free Book Offer, FREEPOST NAT 10298, Richmond, TW9 1BR

Offer valid in UK only and is not available to current Mills & Boon Book Club subscribers to this series. Overseas and Eire please write for details.. We reserve the right to refuse an application and applicants must be aged 18 years or over. Only one application per household. Terms and prices subject to change without notice. Offer expires 31st July 2010. As a result of this application, you may receive offers from Harlequin Mills & Boon and other carefully selected companies. If you would prefer not to share in this opportunity please write to The Data Manager, PO Box 676, Richmond, TW9 1WU.

Mills & Boon® is a registered trademark owned by Harlequin Mills & Boon Limited.
Special Moments™ is being used as a trademark.
The Mills & Boon® Book Club™ is being used as a trademark.